MW01674452

George Fre

The Witness of the Eucharist

SALZWASSER
VERLAG

George Frederick Maclear

The Witness of the Eucharist

Reprint of the original, first published in 1864.

1st Edition 2022 | ISBN: 978-3-75259-540-6

Verlag (Publisher): Salzwasser Verlag GmbH, Zeilweg 44, 60439 Frankfurt, Deutschland
Vertretungsberechtigt (Authorized to represent): E. Roepke, Zeilweg 44, 60439 Frankfurt, Deutschland
Druck (Print): Books on Demand GmbH, In de Tarpen 42, 22848 Norderstedt, Deutschland

The Witness of the Eucharist.

THE

WITNESS OF THE EUCHARIST,

OR

THE INSTITUTION AND EARLY CELEBRATION OF THE LORD'S SUPPER

CONSIDERED AS AN EVIDENCE OF THE HISTORICAL TRUTH OF THE GOSPEL NARRATIVE AND OF THE CHRISTIAN DOCTRINE OF THE ATONEMENT.

BEING THE NORRISIAN PRIZE ESSAY FOR THE YEAR 1863.

BY

THE REV. G. F. MACLEAR, M.A

Cambridge and London.

1864.

"JOHN NORRIS, Esq., the Founder of the Divinity Professorship, by his Will bequeathed a premium of 12*l.* per annum, 7*l.* 4*s.* of which is to be expended upon a gold medal, the residue in books, to the author of the best prose Essay on a sacred subject, which is to be proposed by the Norrisian Professor."

By a Statute approved by Her Majesty by order in Council, April 6, 1858, the Prize is now "given once in five years only, and shall be the sum of the annuities of the five years preceding the adjudication. The Candidates are required to be Graduates of the University of Cambridge, and of not more than thirteen years' standing from admission to their first degrees when the Essays are sent in."

SYNOPSIS OF CONTENTS.

CHAPTER I.

Phenomena of Christian Worship.

PAGE

I. Cessation of the sacrifice of piacular victims 1, 2

II. Celebration during the last 1800 years of a single Rite which alone approximates to the ancient sacrificial ritual .... 4—7

III. The origin of this Rite nowhere explained except in the Gospel Narrative 7

The Account there given .... 8—11

CHAPTER II.

The Religious Revolution thus Attested.

I. The most powerful emotion of which the ancient sacrifices were the expression was a sense of sin ... 13

II. During the last 1800 years this sense of sin instead of being obliterated has gained a stronger hold of the minds of men .... 13—15

PAGE

III. And yet the ancient sacrificial ritual has never been revived! 16, 17

IV. And a Rite presenting a mysterious simplicity in its outward symbols has absorbed the old sacrificial terms, and claims to embody their fulfilment! ...... 18—21

V. And this it has done though its Institutor, by the testimony of friends and enemies, died the death of the malefactor and the slave 22, 23

CHAPTER III.

Alleged Explanations of this Religious Revolution.

This Revolution imperatively calls for some explanation ... 25

I. Can it be ascribed to *Imposture?* .... 26—28

II. Can it be ascribed to *Enthusiasm?* 28

Popular expectations of the Messiah developed in

(1) The Apocalyptic literature of the pre-Christian era 29, 30

(2) The Gospel Narrative 30, 31

(3) The writings of Josephus 32, 33

III. Can it be ascribed to a gradually developed *Mythology?*

Difficulties of this view .... 34—37

Total and overmastering change of religious opinion which the Eucharist pre-supposes .... 38—43

CHAPTER IV.

Examination of the Gospel Narrative.

I. The conditions on which alone the celebration of the Eucharist by Jews can be accounted for .... 45—47

PAGE

II. Does the Gospel Narrative supply these conditions?... 48

III. Harmony and consistency of the Intimation of the Passion ... 49

(a) The Name Jesus as announced to Joseph ... 50
Inferences therefrom ... 51

(b) The words of Simeon ... 52

(c) The witness of the Baptist, *Behold the Lamb of God* ... 54—60

IV. Retrospect of the predictions of a Suffering Messiah in the Old Testament ... 61, 62

Their gradual and progressive character ... 62

A gradual revelation of the same in the New is not, therefore, to be ascribed to an *afterthought* or *change of plan* ... 63, 64

CHAPTER V.

The Early Public Ministry.

I. The First Passover.

(a) First Visit to the Temple ... 66, 67

Sign given to the Jews, *Destroy this Temple and in three days I will raise it up* ... 68, 69

(b) The Visit of Nicodemus ... 70, 71

As Moses lifted up the Serpent in the wilderness, so must the Son of Man be lifted up 72—74

II. The Second Passover.

(c) Feeding of the Five Thousand ... 75—77

The Discourse in the Synagogue of Capernaum ... 78—83

III. Congruity of these Intimations with one another ... 84—86

CHAPTER VI.

THE LATER MINISTRY.

		PAGE
I.	Change in the Intimations now made	87
	(a) The Conversation near Cæsarea Philippi	88, 89
	(b) The Transfiguration	91—94
II.	Further Intimations	96, 97
III.	The last Journey to Jerusalem	100
	(a) The Anointing at Bethany	101, 102
	(b) The Triumphal Entry	104
	(c) The Enquiring Greeks	105—108

CHAPTER VII.

THE INSTITUTION OF THE EUCHARIST.

I.	Characteristics of the Paschal Festival	111—113
II.	Mode of celebration in our Lord's time	113—116
III.	The Preparations for the Last Supper	117—120
IV.	The Institution of the Eucharist	120—122
	Its harmony with all previous announcements of the Passion	123, 124
V.	Reflections on the demeanour of the Saviour at the Institution	124—128
VI.	Conduct of the Apostles during the Crucifixion	128
	The Resurrection alone (1) explains their subsequent conduct	129—134
	(2) gives an adequate account of the celebration of the Eucharist	135—138

CHAPTER VIII.

THE EUCHARIST A SACRIFICIAL FEAST.

PAGE

I. The Eucharist a witness to the *sacrificial* character of the death of Christ .... 139—141

II. Unaccountable if that death was merely a martyrdom 141, 142

III. Reflections on the Institutional Words .... 142—145

Their sacrificial character.................................... 145—147

IV. The Eucharist regarded as a Feast on a Sacrifice by the Early Christians 148

The doctrine of St Paul in 1 Cor. x. 14—21............ 149—152

Necessary inferences therefrom .... 153—158

CHAPTER IX.

THE EUCHARIST A SACRAMENT OF OUR REDEMPTION.

Spirit in which the consideration of the Sacrifice of Christ ought to be approached.. 160

I. The various prophetic intimations of the Messiah in the Old Testament.. 160, 161

II. The varied images employed in the Gospel Narrative to unfold the purport of His death................. 161

III. And again in the teaching of the Apostles 162, 163

PAGE

IV. Similar wise variety in the language of the Church of England .... 164—166

V. The Eucharist an effectual sign of God's goodwill ... 167

VI. Man's need of external symbols .... 168—172

VII. Adaptation of the Eucharist to human wants .... 174—177

CHAPTER I.

PHENOMENA OF CHRISTIAN WORSHIP.

Παρῄνουν γὰρ...καταφρονεῖν βωμῶν, οὓς οἱ πατέρες αὐτῶν καὶ οἱ πρόγονοι πάντες ἐθεράπευσαν.

S. CHRYSOSTOM.

A LATE writer[1] has made some striking observations on the emotions with which a Hebrew of the days of Aaron, Solomon, or Herod would regard the mode of religious worship which now obtains among all Christian nations. Of the many peculiarities which would arrest his attention, none, we may be certain, would be more striking than the entire absence of all such sacrifices as those with which he had been familiar from earliest childhood; in the midst of which he had lived, and moved, and had his being; and without which he could not even conceive the possibility of religious worship at all. Nor would the same peculiarity be less perplexing to a Gentile of the days of Pericles or Alexander, of Cato or Augustus.

To ourselves, indeed, living in a Christian land, the phenomenon is one which presents no difficulty or singularity. On the contrary, during the last eighteen

[1] Professor Wilson in his *Five Gateways of Knowledge.*

hundred years, the world has put on such an altered appearance in reference to the sacrificial ritual that once so universally prevailed, that it actually requires no inconsiderable effort to realize the idea of those sacrifices, which for long ages was in all nations the accepted method of approaching the Supreme Being, under whatever form He was conceived, and with whatever attributes He was clothed.

It is true that the traveller in distant lands will behold relics of this once universal ritual, will see the stricken victim laid upon the altar, the blood poured out, and the worshippers feeding on a portion of the sacrifice. But in all countries calling themselves Christian, that is to say, amongst all the most enlightened and cultivated nations of the present day, such rites have not only ceased, but, in spite of all the violent religious reactions that have since occurred, have never, as a form of national worship, been even partially revived[1].

Now it requires but the slenderest acquaintance with human nature to be aware how long and how pertinaciously old ideas, habits, and associations retain their ascendancy over the mind; and of all ideas, of all

[1] No peculiarity of early Christian worship offended the heathens more than this absence of sacrifice. Comp. Origen, *c. Celsum*, VIII. 17; Arnobius, *adv. Nat.* VI. 1; Minucius Felix, X. 1. The constant source of surprise was "Cur nullas aras habent, templa nulla?" In this respect they contrast Christianity with Judaism: "Judæorum sola et misera gentilitas unum et ipsi Deum, sed palam, sed templis, sed *aris*, *victimis*, cæremoniisque coluerunt." See also S. Chrysostom, *contr. Jud. et Gent.* I. 703 D.

habits, of all associations, none more than those which affect man as a religious being. And yet we have only to look around us to find ourselves confronted with one of the most remarkable religious revolutions that history records. An institution has ceased which the oldest Book in the world reveals as prevailing in the very infancy of the human race, and which was equally accepted by the sweet Psalmist of Israel, the Greek philosopher, and the Roman magistrate; which was once inextricably entwined[1] with all the more solemn epochs in man's domestic life, birth, and marriage[2], and death; with all the most momentous acts in his national and political life, the foundation of cities, the ratification of treaties, the declaration of war; with all the most powerful emotions of his personal and religious life, his hopes and fears, his seasons of joy and sorrow, his hours of despondency, his sense of guilt, his craving after restoration to the Divine favour. An institution has ceased which was once celebrated with all the pomp of ceremonial ritual, and gave employment to thousands and tens of thousands of the priestly order in the Mosaic Tabernacle, in the statelier structures of Solomon and Herod, in the graceful shrines of classic Greece, in the massive temples of imperial Rome, amidst the stone circles of the Celtic Druid, and under

[1] See Archbp. Thomson's *Bampton Lectures*, p. 43; Döllinger's *Gentile and Jew*, II. 80.

[2] For the sacrifices at Greek marriages, see Becker's *Charicles*, p. 353, and the passages there quoted; Döllinger's *Gentile and Jew*, II. 80.

the solemn oak-groves of the Saxon and the Northman; in fact, amongst all nations and peoples, though in well-nigh every other respect—habits, institutions, ideas, and modes of life—sundered from one another as widely as the poles[1].

That a system once so universal, once so potent, has utterly ceased among Christian nations, is an historical fact brought home to us by our daily experience. The sacrifice of 'bulls and goats,' the confession over them of guilt and shortcoming, the slaughtering of them before the altar, the sprinkling of the offerers with the blood, these ceremonies once of daily, hourly occurrence throughout the whole world, are with us entirely matters of the past, and when they meet us in Jewish history, the poems of Homer, or the narrative of Livy, are so alien from anything we now see around us, that we have a difficulty in even satisfactorily and

[1] "'The Mahometan religion,' says Gibbon, as if in praise of its purity, 'has no Priest and no Sacrifice.' This statement must be considerably qualified. Sacrifice, though it forms no part of the daily worship in the mosque, yet on solemn occasions is an essential element of the Mussulman ritual. It is generally, if not universally, of the nature of a thank-offering, and, as in the case of most ancient sacrifices, is combined with an act of benevolence to the poor. To the Bedouin Arabs it is almost their only act of devotion. It was only under the pretext of sacrificing on the tomb of Aaron that Burckhardt was able to enter Petra. The railroad, recently opened from the Danube to the Black Sea, was inaugurated by the sacrifice of two sheep. The vast slaughter of victims at Mecca is the only scene now existing in the world that recalls the ancient sacrifices of Jew or Pagan. In short, it might be said that, so far from Mahometanism being the only religion without a sacrifice, it is the only civilized religion that retains a sacrifice, not spiritually or mystically, but in the literal ancient sense." Dean Stanley's *Eastern Church*, p. 276, also *Lectures on Jewish History*, 168.

clearly realizing the fact that they ever obtained among men.

This singular revolution in the religious life of the most civilized nations of the present day is a fact which none can gainsay or dispute, and of itself claims some adequate and consistent explanation.

But side by side with this cessation of a system once so universal, there is another no less striking peculiarity of Christian worship. In the place of a complex sacrificial ritual hallowed by the associations of centuries, and the memories of man since the infancy of the human race, a single Rite has been received and uninterruptedly celebrated during the last eighteen hundred years, which alone approximates in the slightest degree to that system which has passed away. Though, to the outward senses at least, this rite is of the simplest possible character, it is yet celebrated in every part of Europe, and amongst all Christian nations whether in Asia, Africa, or America; it has survived the most numerous and diverse changes of manners, habits, and modes of thought; it has seen the rise, progress, and decay of countless theories, opinions, and philosophies; it is observed by Churches differing from one another, and that sometimes with the greatest bitterness, not only in respect to other rites and ceremonies, but also in 'matters of faith;' and whether it be celebrated with an almost rude simplicity, or with all the accessories of pomp and ceremony, it has not only absorbed all the terms and expressions once employed in reference to the old sacrificial system, but has met and satisfied all those deep emotions of the human breast which that system once attracted.

And what are 'the outward and visible signs' of this Rite? *Bread and wine, which are eaten and drunk by the worshippers.* Now it is true that the reception of these elements accompanied and formed part of Jewish, and, in a certain sense, of Gentile sacrifices[1], but such reception always presupposed the offering of some victim. And the mere fact that these elements should now be received separately and detached from what always accompanied them, and gave them their distinctive value, is, to say the least, a very striking circumstance, and lends a peculiar interest to our inquiry into the origin of this Rite.

Now of its origin all the Christian Churches, differing as they do from one another in other respects, have agreed to receive one single account and no other; they have from the beginning referred its institution to one and the same period of time, to one and the same Person. Nor is their testimony contradicted by heathen

[1] 'Simple breaking of bread with sacrificial intent and gesture was a sufficient "immolation," simple pouring out of wine with that intent was effective "mactation" of the yet living victim.' Freeman's *Principles of Divine Service*, II. 81. 'The victim though itself the efficacious element of the sacrifice, was offered *by means of the bread and wine.* The bread was broken and sprinkled on the head of the animal while yet alive; and again wine, with frankincense, was poured between its horns. This done, the sacrifice was conceived to have been duly offered, so far as concerned the *gift* and dedication of it on man's part, and the acceptance of it by the Deity. This is proved by the fact that *immolare*, to sprinkle with the broken *mola*, or cake, was used, as is well known, to express the *entire action of sacrifice*, the slaying and burning included.' Ibid. p. 76.

writers who lived about or shortly after the time of its institution. The brief and incidental notices of the life of the Institutor which occur in Tacitus[1] or Josephus[2], in Suetonius[3] or Pliny[4], so far as they go, entirely bear out the account which all the Christian Churches from the first day until now with one voice have agreed to accept. And what are the facts thus mutually corroborated?

That the Institutor of this Rite appeared about 1864 years ago, during the reigns of the Emperors Augustus and Tiberius, in Judæa, a comparatively unknown and obscure corner of the vast Roman Empire; that He was of the humblest origin, and drew around Him a small body of equally humble disciples, by whom He was looked up to as their Teacher; that by the great body of His nation He was rejected and despised, and His teaching regarded as blasphemous; that He was put to death at the instigation of that nation by the procurator Pontius Pilate, and underwent the punishment of crucifixion, the ignominious doom of the malefactor and the slave[5].

[1] *Annal.* XV. 44.

[2] *Antiq.* XVIII. 3. 3; F. H. Schoedel (*Vindiciæ Flavianæ*, Lips. 1840) contends for the genuineness of the whole passage in Josephus. See Kurtz's *Church History*, p. 61.

[3] *In Claudio*, c. XXV. Comp. Juv. *Sat.* I. 155.

[4] Letter to Trajan. Compare also the letter of Mara to Serapion, Cureton, *Spicil. Syriacum*, Lond. 1855; Milman's *Bampton Lectures*, 20.

[5] 'We have the plain testimonies of the greatest enemies of Christianity, that there was such a person as Christ, who suffered according to the Scripture story. For Tacitus not only mentions the Christians as

About these facts there never has been any dispute. There exists no trace or vestige of any record either contemporary with the institution of this Rite, or which has come to light since, that gives a substantially different account of the life and death of the Institutor.

It appears, then, not only that a time-honoured system of religious worship has utterly disappeared among all civilized nations; not only that the single Rite which in the slightest degree approximates to that system is, to the outward sense, of the most mysterious simplicity, as compared with the elaborate and multiform ceremonies it has displaced; but that it was instituted by One, who died a most degrading death, and that it commemorates, or 'shows forth' that death, as often as it is celebrated.

For not only are the elements of Bread and Wine eaten and drunk by the worshippers, but, in spite of the degradation they involve, the circumstances of the original institution are every time rehearsed in their ears. Every time they receive these elements, they hear in the language of the only account of the Institution which the Universal Church has agreed to accept, that,

suffering at Rome for their religion in the time of Nero, but saith, That the Author of this religion was one Christ, who suffered under Pontius Pilate, Procurator of Judea, in the time of Tiberius, which is an irrefragable testimony of the truth of the story concerning Christ, in an age, when, if it had been false, nothing could have been more easily detected than such a fiction, by the number of Jews which were continually at Rome; and neither Julian, nor Celsus, nor Porphyry, nor Lucian did ever question the truth of the story itself, but only upbraided the Christians for attributing too much to Christ.' Stillingfleet's *Letter to a Deist, Works*, Vol. II. 130.

on the night before He died, and in the certain prospect of that death, so cruel and so shameful, the Institutor, so far from being perturbed or alarmed thereat, at a Paschal Supper in company with twelve of His immediate followers, '*Took Bread, blessed it, brake it, and distributed it to them, saying, Take, eat, this is My Body, which is given for you; likewise He took a Cup of Wine, and when He had given thanks He gave it unto them, saying, This is My Blood of the new Covenant, which is shed for you and for many, for the remission of sins; Do this, as oft as ye shall drink it, in remembrance of Me.*'

And yet, though the Institutor of this Rite did die on the day after by this ignominious death[1], though during His life His Name was not known beyond the limits of the obscurest corner of the Roman Empire, though He had 'no victories, no conquests, no revolutions, no surprising elevation of fortune, no achievements of valour, of strength, or of policy, to appeal to, no discoveries in any art or science, no great efforts of genius or learning to produce[2],' though He lived and moved in the humblest station, and save to very few was known only as the son of a carpenter of Nazareth; though His followers were for many years regarded as the scum and offscouring of the earth, were reviled, mocked, perse-

[1] 'Hominem summo supplicio perditum.' Minucius Felix, chap. IX. Comp. Tac. *Ann.* XV. 44; Arnob. *adv. Gentes*, I. 20; Lactantius, *Div. Inst.* IV. 26, 29; S. Chrysostom, *contra Jud. et Gentiles*, I. 683 A; 696 A; 698 C; 702 C.

[2] Paley's *Evidences*, chap. VI.

cuted, and in many instances put to death with revolting barbarity; in spite of all this, they not only never concealed the fact that He, from whom they were called Christians, died a violent and ignominious death, but preached it openly, wherever they could find men to listen to the story, and celebrated this Rite with feelings of the deepest reverence and adoration, and with emotions such as they had never felt before, save when they were present at the most august ceremonies of that sacrificial ritual under which they had been brought up from earliest childhood.

Nay, more; in spite of every adverse influence which their own obscurity or the open hostility of the whole power of the Roman Empire could bring to bear upon them, the first disciples of the Institutor of this Rite succeeded in obtaining its observance wherever they went. Their tenets spread with unexampled rapidity[1] throughout the Roman Empire, and in spite of contempt and outrage commended themselves to the hearts of men. Philosophers might scoff at the first believers; politicians might suspect them; the populace might pursue them with ferocious yells; successive emperors might pour upon them the fury of their anger, but the new Faith won its way; what at first had been the consolation of the slave or the fugitive in the catacombs, became the creed of the statesman and the

[1] Ἀναλόγισαι, πόσοι δόγματα ἠβουλήθησαν εἰσαγαγεῖν παρ' Ἕλλησι, καὶ πολιτείαν ἐνστήσασθαι ξένην, οἷον Ζήνων, Πλάτων, Σωκράτης, Διαγόρας, Πυθαγόρας, καὶ ἕτεροι μύριοι· ἀλλ' ὅμως τοσοῦτον ἀπέσχον περιγενέσθαι, ὡς μηδὲ ἐξ ὀνόματος εἶναι τοῖς πολλοῖς γνώριμοι. S. Chrysostom *adv. Judæos, Op.* I. 770 A.

magistrate, and from that day to this a Rite, which, under its simplest and most obvious aspect, 'sets forth' and commemorates the cruel and ignominious death of its Institutor, has been uninterruptedly celebrated, and regarded as the most solemn ordinance of their religion by all orders and degrees of men.

CHAPTER II.

THE RELIGIOUS REVOLUTION THUS ATTESTED.

Τὴν μνήμην τοῦ μεγάλου θύματος.

EUSEBIUS.

BEFORE proceeding to an examination of the causes that can be assigned for this unparalleled revolution in the religious history of mankind, there are one or two additional points bearing on what has been said in the preceding Chapter which are deserving of attention.

Without opening the controverted question as to the origin of the sacrificial ritual which once so universally obtained throughout the world, or attempting any precise analysis of the motives that led to its observance, it may be asserted, without fear of contradiction, that in their most general acceptation sacrifices were 'gifts by means of which man strove to make good his imperfect consecration of himself to God, who is his lawful Lord[1].' They were based on a sense, more or less vivid, of imperfection, of a gulf fixed between the offerer and God; and their general prevalence over the heathen

[1] See Archbp. Thomson's *Bampton Lectures*, p. 31.

world, proves, in the language of Bishop Butler, that 'the idea of repentance being sufficient to expiate guilt, is contrary to the general sense of mankind[1].'

Now, no one will venture to account for the cessation of the ancient sacrificial system on the ground that man's sense of personal imperfection, and his consciousness of sin have ceased also, or disappeared like the phantoms of a troubled dream[2]. So far is this from being so, that it may be safely affirmed that there never was a time when these emotions have more powerfully and more generally affected the human heart than during the last eighteen hundred years.

The very words '*sin*' and '*transgression*' have acquired a meaning infinitely deeper and more searching than they ever bore in the mouths of the wisest of the great moral teachers of Greece and Rome[3]. A code of morality has been promulgated, and has been accepted by the most civilized nations, which deepens and intensifies the sternest demands of the Mosaic law, and brings out as was never brought out before, the infinite distance between the creature and an all-pure Creator. Words such as were certainly never before spoken by man have been reverberating through the last eighteen centuries, demanding the obedience not

[1] Butler's *Analogy*, Part II. chap. 5.

[2] The great exception to the practice of sacrifice is in the system of Buddhism, 'but along with sacrifice, Buddhism rejects the notion that lay at the root of it, namely, that past sin presents any objective obstacle to the sinner's return to God.' See Macdonnel's *Donnellan Lectures*, p. 90 and note XXIV. Archbp. Thomson's *Bampton Lectures*, note 30, p. 264.

[3] See Archbp. Trench's *New Testament Synonyms*, Part II. p. 63.

merely of the hand or the head but of the heart, and tracing all shortcoming to the inmost recesses of the conscience. A Voice has been heard, saying,

It was said by them of old time, Thou shalt not kill, and whosoever shall kill shall be in danger of the judgment: but I say unto you, That whosoever is angry with his brother without a cause shall be in danger of the judgment, and whosoever shall say to his brother, Raca, shall be in danger of the council, but whosoever shall say, Thou fool, shall be in danger of hell-fire[1].

It was said by them of old time, Thou shalt not commit adultery: but I say unto you, That whosoever looketh on a woman to lust after her has committed adultery already with her in his heart[2].

It hath been said, Thou shalt love thy neighbour, and hate thine enemy: but I say unto you, Love your enemies, bless them that curse you, do good to them that hate you, and pray for them that despitefully use you and persecute you[3].

There is nothing from without a man, that entering into him can defile him: but the things which come out of him, those are they that defile the man...for from within, out of the heart of men, proceed evil thoughts, adulteries, fornications, murders, thefts, covetousness, wickedness, deceit, lasciviousness, an evil eye, blasphemy, pride, foolishness: all these things come from within, and defile the man[4].

[1] Matt. v. 21, 22.
[2] Matt. v. 27, 28.
[3] Matt. v. 43, 44.
[4] Mark vii. 15, 21—23.

This Voice has not only been heard, but it has convinced successive generations of men of their shortcomings, of the great gulf between them and that righteousness which alone can be acceptable in the sight of the All-holy. They have agreed to listen to that Voice, and however much in actual fact they may fail to conform to its requirements, it has been ever accepted as exhibiting the standard of morality to which they feel bound to aspire.

On the authority, morever, of the same Voice, it has been the universal belief of mankind in all Christian countries, that life has an awful and mysterious importance, that it is but the portal of another life, that at the close of the present order of things mankind are to be judged according to the deeds done in the body, whether they be good or whether they be evil, and that on this judgment depend the most tremendous issues whether of happiness or of misery for all time to come. We do not affirm that this article of the faith, for it is to be found in every Christian creed, has had anything like that *due* and *adequate* effect on the lives and actions of men which it ought to have had. But an influence such as was never seen before the Christian era it certainly has exerted. In combination with other causes it has gone far to foster a national conscience, and to deepen the sense of individual responsibility for sins not merely of the hand and mouth, but of the heart and thoughts, so that there never was a time when sin was less generally regarded with indifference, or the consciousness thereof deemed an illusion and an infirmity. There never was a time when, in spite of his best actions, the utter inability of man alone and unaided to satisfy the just requirements of his Maker was more generally felt. Martyrs, the most noble and heroic, have borne all the agonies of the most refined torture with unflinching fortitude, and holy men and women, in poverty and obscurity, have yielded up their lives to death, and with their latest breath have declared that in themselves 'dwelt no good thing,' that they were after all but 'unprofitable servants.' 'God be merciful to me a sinner' is the leading idea of the inscriptions on thousands of gravestones in the stately cathedral and the village churchyard, and bears silent testimony to the deepest convictions of mankind.

And yet, though this is the case, those propitiatory sacrifices once multiplied by the sons of men, especially in seasons of national or domestic calamity, with frightful prodigality[1], have utterly ceased. Though the sense of guilt, which prompted so many sacrifices, and in the case of the Jewish nation called forth a peculiar and

[1] Thus Augustus and Marcus Aurelius required so great a number of beasts for their sacrifices that it was said *All oxen and calves hoped and prayed that they might never return from their journeys, or campaigns, as otherwise they were infallibly lost.* Seneca *de Benef.* III. 2. At the accession of Caligula 160,000 victims were slaughtered, and the same Emperor had innocent men dressed out as victims, and then thrown down precipices, as an atonement for his life. Suet. *Cal.* XIV. In the time of Domitian the cities of the Hellespont being alarmed by an earthquake, public and private resources were drained to offer a very special and secret sacrifice to Poseidon. Döllinger, II. 176, 180. The annual sprinkling of the image of Jupiter Latiaris was of regular occurrence even in the 2nd and 3rd centuries A.D. Minucius Felix, XXI. 30.

special class of sacrifices[1], viz. sin and trespass offerings, has been deepened and intensified to a degree even Mosaism scarcely knew, yet the ancient sacrificial ritual has never succeeded in regaining its hold! Though in the main, man is now what he was during the ages anterior to Christianity, though he is still a being subject to all the vicissitudes of earthly existence, though he still 'cometh up, and is cut down like a flower,' has 'still but a short time to live, and is full of misery,' though he is still sensible of all the profound emotions which once called forth the ancient sacrifices, and even prompted man to give *the fruit of his body for the sin of his soul*, though in his efforts to rid himself of the consciousness of personal shortcoming he has from time to time resorted to the wildest religious extravagances and voluntarily submitted to the most painful self-torture—yet he has never sought relief in a system which for four thousand years was universally recognised as the proper external means for making good man's imperfect consecration of himself to God.

Now it will not be denied that this constitutes the most singular feature of the religious revolution which has taken place. If sacrificial observances formed, as we know they did, an invariable part of ancient religious worship, when the sense of sin was *confessedly weak*, how is it that when it has been so *deepened and intensified* the old sacrificial ritual has not revived? If it be said that legislative decrees repressed them, that the sentiment of mankind was gradually alienated from

[1] See Kurtz's *Sacrificial System*, p. 197, E.T.

them, we reply by asking not only how comes it to pass that legislation[1], in religious matters so notoriously weak and incompetent, has *succeeded* in banishing so effectually such a time-honoured system, but whence came the spirit that *inspired* that legislation, what *powerful* causes, and they must certainly have been *very* powerful, which were able to produce such a surprising revolution in the sentiment of mankind?

But if the ancient sacrificial system has disappeared, in spite of the deeper sense of individual responsibility for sins even of the thoughts which has taken hold of the world, and in spite, too, of the belief which has grown up of a terrible and just judgment to be meted out to every man hereafter 'according to the deeds done in the body,' what has become of the old sacrificial phraseology, of the words and phrases which for generation and generation men were wont to use when speaking of the objects at which they aimed when presenting their various sacrifices? Have such expressions as 'victim' and 'offering,' 'oblation' and 'satisfaction,' 'propitiation' and 'atonement' vanished from the language of Christian nations? Do we find them like fossils in the Mosaic law, or trace them only in the pages of the great heathen writers? Have they fallen out of the Christian vocabulary, or retired from it as expressive of worn-out and useless ideas and conceptions? Or have they found a centre to which to attach themselves, an historical fact with which to associate?

[1] On the decree of Theodosius, A.D. 381, against sacrifice, see Gibbon, III. 413. Smith's Ed.

From the first hour of its institution to the present, they have never failed to be associated with that ordinance to which reference has been made in the preceding Chapter, and with the death it 'sets forth' and commemorates[1]. For though they who first celebrated this Rite, and handed it down to us, were not only not philosophers, or men of great mental attainments, but poor and illiterate; though they had from their earliest childhood lived and moved amidst the old sacrificial system; though from habit, from association, from predilection, they would have been naturally inclined to maintain that system, and vehemently opposed to its abolition; they yet never faltered in their declaration that that system was not so much abolished, as perfectly and completely *fulfilled*, realized, and accomplished by the death which the Institutor of this Rite underwent; and they transfer to it, not with *careful* and *elaborate explanations*, not with *doubt* and *hesitation* as to their propriety, not as though they were using *strange language incapable of being understood by their contemporaries*, but *naturally, unaffectedly,* and *without strain or effort*, words and phrases once exclusively employed in the vocabulary of that sacrificial system which has so marvellously disappeared. Thus in a letter, the authenticity of which has never been disputed[2], written to the Church of Corinth, in or near the year A.D. 57, that is,

[1] See Waterland on *the Doctrinal Use of the Christian Sacraments*, Works, VIII. 130.

[2] Even Strauss admits the genuineness of St Paul's Epistles. *Leben Jesu*, E. T. I. 60.

only twenty-four years after the death of the Institutor of this Rite, He is called a *Paschal Victim*[1]; in the same letter the writer distinctly compares this Rite with the sacrificial feasts of heathen nations[2]. In another, written in the following year to the same Church, he ascribes to the death thus shown forth *the reconciliation of mankind to God*[3], the very object of the ancient sacrifices. Similar expressions occur in other letters, written not to prove this especial point but on widely-different subjects; while in one addressed to men who had been brought up all their lives under the Mosaic ritual, the same writer, or at least one deeply imbued with his spirit and mode of thought, devotes several chapters to develope the complete fulfilment of that system by the death of the Institutor of this Rite. Thus he repeatedly applies to Him the title of *High-priest*[4]; he draws out in detail a comparison between Him and the Jewish high-priests; he speaks of Him as *entering into the Holy Place with His own blood*[5]; of His *offering Himself without spot unto God*[6], of His being *manifested to put away sin by the sacrifice of Himself*[7], of *His being once offered to bear the sins of many*[8]; he declares that Christians *have an altar of which they might not eat who served the Tabernacle*[9]; he exhorts

[1] 1 Cor. v. 7. [2] 1 Cor. x. 21.

[3] 2 Cor. v. 18, 19; comp. Rom. v. 10, 11. A more specific reference to these passages will be found below in Chap. IX.

[4] Heb. ii. 17; iii. 1; iv. 14; v. 10; vi. 20; viii. 1; ix. 11.

[5] Heb. ix. 12. [6] Heb. ix. 14. [7] Heb. ix. 26. [8] Heb. ix. 28.

[9] Heb. xiii. 10. On θυσιαστήριον as contrasted with βωμός, see Archbp. Trench's *N. T. Synonyms*, 2nd series, pp. 78—80.

his readers to *offer continually the sacrifice of thanksgiving to God through Him, Who, that He might sanctify the people with His own blood, suffered without the gate*[1]. Concurrently with the spontaneous use of this phraseology we find no single precept enjoining the observance of one of the ancient sacrificial ceremonies; but we discover that this Rite was uninterruptedly celebrated, in spite of the mysteriously simple and ordinary features it must have presented to men living in a sacrificial age, and that not after the lapse of centuries, but from the first it gathered to itself and the death it commemorates, the varied conceptions of the old sacrificial terminology. Thus to say nothing of the formal Liturgies which it inspired, we find in the age immediately succeeding that of the first disciples, one writer, about A.D. 95, applying to it the name *Προσφόρα*, or 'oblation[2];' another, about A.D. 107, calls it *Εὐχαριστία*, 'a sacrifice of thanksgiving[3];' another of fifty years afterwards, or A.D. 150, calls it a *Θυσία*, or 'sacrifice[4];' another, about A.D. 250, calls it a *Πάσχα*, or 'Paschal Feast[5].'

Now no one will deny that these names have a clear and distinct reference to sacrificial ideas and conceptions; they are no new names coined now for the first

[1] Heb. xiii. 15, 12.

[2] Clemens Romanus, *Ep.* I. *ad Cor.* c. 44. See Waterland *on the Eucharist*, VII. 26; Guericke's *Antiquities of the Christian Church*, p. 253.

[3] Ignatius, *Ep. ad Smyrn.* VII. VIII. XX. See Dorner *on the Person of Christ*, I. 99.

[4] Justin Martyr, *Dial. cum Tryph.* p. 137.

[5] Origen, *contr. Celsum*, VIII. 759, Ed. Ben.; see Waterland, VII. 41.

time to express thoughts hitherto unknown; they 'belong to a vocabulary of sacrificial language, familiar alike to Jew and Gentile[1],' they are not elaborately and anxiously explained, justified, or defended, as though those who heard them were likely to stand aghast at their appropriation to this Rite; they are enunciated boldly, fearlessly, without dread of the consequences. And who, we ask again, were they that first so applied them? Who were they that initiated this astonishing revolution in the religious observances of mankind? They were not dreamy philosophers elaborating in some calm retreat a scheme to reconcile different religious systems. They were not Jewish priests learned in the ritual of the Law, or prominent members of any great sacerdotal order of the Gentiles. They were twelve humble men, of slender literary attainments, whose lives were all, more or less, one long-continued martyrdom, who had no *time* for philosophical dreaming or speculation, who from the very first day that they began to proclaim their tenets were exposed to the frown of the magistrate and the bigotry of their nation. And their preaching, so far from being regarded as the ravings of enthusiastic dreamers, 'has overcome the world;' has been accepted as containing the 'highest philosophy' by some of the greatest intellects that the world has seen; has brought about the greatest religious revolution of any age; has succeeded in obtaining for a Rite, which, under its first and most obvious aspect,

[1] See Freeman's *Principles of Divine Service*, II. 92.

commemorates an ignominious and cruel death, an uninterrupted celebration for eighteen hundred years, and an attachment so strong that multitudes would rather part with their lives than lose the benefits which they believe to be therein signed and sealed to them.

CHAPTER III.

ALLEGED EXPLANATIONS OF THIS RELIGIOUS REVOLUTION.

῞Οταν γὰρ λέγουσι, πόθεν δῆλον ὅτι ἐτύθη ὁ Χριστός; μετὰ τῶν ἄλλων, καὶ ἀπὸ μυστηρίων αὐτοὺς ἐπιστομίζομεν, εἰ γὰρ μὴ ἀπέθανεν ὁ ᾿Ιησοῦς, τίνος σύμβολα τὰ τελουμένα;—S. CHRYSOSTOM.

FROM what has been advanced, then, in the preceding Chapter, it appears that amongst all Christian nations, that is, among the most civilized nations of the present day, a marvellous revolution in their religious observances has taken place. (i.) For upwards of 4000 years, to adopt the common chronology, there existed among all nations a peculiar mode of approaching the Supreme Being, namely, with the sacrifice of piacular victims. *These sacrifices have entirely disappeared.* (ii.) The most powerful emotion on which they were based was man's sense of imperfection, his consciousness of shortcoming, and a felt necessity for something more than personal repentance to expiate guilt. During the last eighteen hundred years this sense of guilt, instead of being obliterated, has gained a deeper and stronger hold of the minds of men, and that to a greater extent than ever was known before; and yet, *though this is the case, the ancient sacrificial system has never been revived.* (iii.) During the same period a Rite has been uninterruptedly celebrated, presenting in the mysterious simplicity of its 'outward and visible signs' the strongest possible contrast to the ancient sacrificial system, and yet associating with itself the terminology of that system, and claiming to embody its fulfilment. (iv.) It has obtained this uninterrupted and universal celebration, though its Institutor, on the testimony both of friends and enemies, appeared in an obscure corner of the Roman empire, was born in the humblest circumstances, attracted to Himself during His lifetime a few equally humble followers, and having *achieved no victories, having conciliated no prejudices, was, at the instigation of its rulers, put to death, and did actually die the death of the malefactor and the slave.*

For this unparalleled revolution we now seek an adequate and consistent explanation, one, that is, which will harmonise its otherwise startling and contradictory phenomena, and explain how it originated, not, it is to be remembered, at a period so distant as to be lost in a fabulous antiquity, but at '*a period of which we know a great deal, and within historic times*[1].'

These data, then, at once supply us with a test whereby we may measure the adequacy of certain explanations of this revolution which have found more or less numerous advocates.

i. It has been held, then, that it originated in *impos-*

[1] See *Aids to Faith*, p. 71; Rawlinson's *Bampton Lectures*, p. 221.

ture. To the Christian the mere mention of such an opinion is revolting, but it is necessary to revert to it for a few moments. And here it will not be necessary to repeat what has been urged again and again ever since the days of the opponents of Celsus and Julian, or to ask how it is possible that the character of an impostor can be attributed to One whom unbelievers themselves have agreed to recognise as the purest and holiest being that ever lived; whose words and teaching have been regarded as the most exalted and superhuman that the world has ever heard[1]; whose morality has incorporated itself with the civil polity and domestic relations of the most civilized nations of the present day; whose example has covered a considerable portion of the globe with beneficent and philanthropic institutions utterly unknown before He came? Nor, if the charge be shifted to His first disciples, need we ask how it is possible that twelve poor illiterate men can be believed to have leagued themselves together to proclaim to the world a story which they knew to be false; that they should all have unanimously resolved to maintain the same story, and that too based upon the same evidence; that they should have further done this though they had not a single particle of worldly interest therein, and by proclaiming it voluntarily and knowingly exposed themselves to the hostility, the odium, the contempt of their own nation, and brought upon themselves continual

[1] See S. Chrysostom, *adv. Judæos*, *Op.* I. 772 A. Ed. Ben. Also a striking quotation from J. J. Rousseau on the character of Jesus, quoted by Horne in his *Introduction to the Study of the Scriptures*, I. 422.

peril and the constant expectation of a violent death[1]? We need not dwell upon these points, for, besides other reasons, they lie outside the limits of our present argument. We will rather ask whether it is credible that One conscious of such imposture could, a few hours before undergoing a cruel and ignominious death, have not only been exempt from all natural apprehensions respecting it, but have calmly and deliberately instituted a Rite to commemorate and 'shew forth' that death for all future time? We will ask whether it is credible even for a moment that the first disciples could have observed a Rite so instituted in spite of the shame and degradation it implied, and have transferred to the Death it symbolized all those sacrificial expressions and conceptions which they had been wont to connect with an august and elaborate ritual consecrated by the veneration of ages? We will ask whether it is credible that before a Rite so instituted, a time-honoured sacrificial ritual should have gradually disappeared, as history proves it has; and that Christian Churches, though differing from one another in many particulars, and made by their very differences the more jealous guardians of their traditions and ceremonies, should have *unanimously agreed to celebrate it*, and at the same time proclaim with one voice, not that man's consciousness of sin and imperfection is an idle dream, but the stern-

[1] See Stillingfleet's *Orig. Sacræ*, Book II. chap. 9; Milman's *Bampton Lectures*, p. 51. On the contrary argument, that all religions have had their martyrs, see Sherlock's *Trial of the Witnesses*, Works, Vol. IV. pp. 435—8.

est reality—aye, infinitely more real than the greatest moral teachers of Greece and Rome even conceived? When an authenticated instance of men conscious of imposture requiring of their disciples the most exalted morality, and willingly devoting themselves to odium, contempt, danger, and death, can be adduced, then it will be time to consider the opinion that the institution of this mysterious Rite can have originated in imposture, as deserving even of a moment's attention.

ii. But, secondly, it has been held that this revolution originated *in the popular imagination of the era of the Advent, excited by Messianic hopes.* It is asserted that the countrymen and followers of the Institutor of this Rite were strongly prepossessed by the national expectations of a coming Messiah, and that His appearance, His teaching, His spotless life so won upon them, that after His death they believed Him to be the promised Messiah, and celebrated His memory accordingly[1].

It may be well, therefore, in dealing with this opinion, to inquire briefly what were the expectations of the person or work of the Messiah at the time when the Institutor of this Rite appeared. That from the earliest period of their national history the Jews had been pre-eminently 'the people of the future,' that they were at the period in question filled with the hope that an extraordinary Being should appear and realize the idea of a Messiah or Deliverer, is conceded on all sides. Now the characteristics they chiefly attributed to Him were

[1] See Mill's *Pantheism*, p. 85; Ebrard's *Gospel Narrative*, p. 24.

regal, and prophetic. They looked for a great Conqueror, whom God would send; they invested Him with the attributes of majesty and humanity; they described Him as the 'Elect One,' 'the Anointed,' the 'Son of Man,' the 'King from the sons of Jesse,' who 'should execute a terrible vengeance on the enemies of His people,' who should 'go forth from them, and be revealed from the midst of them, and teach them the worship of the Lord[1].' But we search the Apocalyptic literature of the pre-Christian era, and the Targums[2] contemporary with that era, alike in vain for any clear recognition of the fact that the work of the Messiah would have any definite relation to the ancient sacrificial system, or prepare for its cessation. A single fragment of the popular literature, though 'distinguished from the Apocalyptic writings by a clearer recognition of the sins of the people,' and exhibiting more fully the spiritual character of the reign of the Messiah, betrays an expectation that 'he will bruise unjust rulers,' 'cleanse Jerusalem,' 'remove sinners,' 'shake the earth with his word,' 'bless His people,' and 'rule over the Gentiles;' but the idea that *He will die does not once occur;* and so far from there being any trace in early Jewish writings of a belief in 'the substitution of a spiritual for a ritual law[3],' the object of their highest hopes is the

[1] See Westcott's *Introduction to the New Testament*, pp. 92, 95, and the quotations from the 'Book of Henoch,' and the 'Sibylline Oracles;' Ebrard, p. 486.

[2] On the ideas of the Messiah's Person and Work in the Targums, see Ebrard, 487.

[3] Westcott, p. 123, n.

'permanent establishment of the Law as the rule of the whole earth[1].' The idea of a temporal king, fighting and conquering, and exalting the nation above all other nations, recurs again and again in the literature of this era, 'and perfectly coincides with what we know of the disposition of the Jewish people at this period, with the material character of their hopes, with their exclusive preoccupation about the temporal and political work of the Messiah, and finally with their immoderate predilection for the doctrine of angels and demons[2].'

Exactly similar are the inferences we gather from the popular expectations of the Messiah, so far as we obtain glimpses of them in the Gospel narrative and the writings of Josephus. Everywhere, we learn, there was a feverish anxiety respecting the coming of the Messiah. The appearance of the Baptist at the banks of Jordan, recalling by his garb and preaching the old prophets, was the signal for all Jerusalem, Judea, and the country round about to flock to His baptism, musing whether he were the Messiah or no[3]. It was the opinion of the national teachers that His coming would be heralded by Elias, and the belief was shared by the

[1] 'It was a common and generally received opinion among the Jewish nation, that Messiah when He came should no whit alter, much less abolish any of their Mosaic ordinances, but should enhance them to a greater glory. That He should make their sacrifices, purifications, sabbaths, festivals, and all other usances, far more resplendent and glorious than ever they had been.' Lightfoot's Sermons, *Works*, p. 1045, folio edition.

[2] Pressense's *Religions before Christ*, 235, 6.

[3] John i. 41; Matt. iii. 5; Luke iii. 15; John iii. 26; Luke xvii. 20.

common people[1]; but there was considerable uncertainty as to the manner of His appearance, *when Christ cometh*, said the people of Jerusalem, *no man knoweth whence He is*[2]. It was, however, regarded as certain that He should be born at Bethlehem, the city of David[3]; that He should be David's son[4], and should sit on David's throne; that He should *abide for ever*, and set up a kingdom in which He would dispense honours on *His right hand and on His left*[5]. With these regal characteristics of His person and work others combined prophetic functions, and looked for *the Prophet that should come into the world*[6], expecting from Him signs not unlike the giving of the manna in the wilderness, and instruction *in all things*[7]. But whether their anticipations fastened most fondly on His regal or prophetic characteristics, the idea that He would ever suffer or die *never once occurs.* Though in the Temple of Prophecy there had from the beginning ever been heard two Voices mysteriously blended, one jubilant and glad, telling of victory and of triumph, and the other mournful and subdued, whispering of shame and suffering, yet to one of these Voices only had attention ever been paid; and it was resolutely maintained that these prophecies of a suffering 'servant

[1] Matt. xvii. 10 and the parallels; comp. also xvi. 14.

[2] John vii. 27.

[3] Matt. ii. 5; comp. John vii. 41, 42.

[4] Comp. Matt. xxii. 42; xii. 23; ix. 27; xx. 30; xv. 22; xxi. 9.

[5] Matt. xx. 21; Mark x. 37.

[6] Comp. John vi. 14, with which comp. John i. 21, 46; vii. 40; 1 Macc. xiv. 41.

[7] John iv. 25.

of God' applied to the nation or the heathen[1], or that there would be two Messiahs, the one to suffer, the other to triumph. In complete harmony with this we find that during His lifetime, the disciples of the Institutor of this Rite shrunk with horror and amazement from the idea that He ever could die[2], up to the last moment could not bring themselves to believe that such an event ever would come to pass, and, when it did come to pass, deemed every hope lost, and every expectation disappointed[3]. As for the idea that by His death He would inaugurate a new cycle of history, or that the old sacrificial system would pass away, we do not find a single trace of anything approaching to it in the Gospel narrative as forming part of the national expectation of the Messiah's work. On the contrary, if there was a zealous determination to maintain one thing more than another, it was the Law with its ritual and its ordinances. The true popular idea of the Messiah receives illustration from the writings of Josephus, and is realized in such men as the Sorcerer, who, during the procuratorship of Fadus, persuaded the great mass of the people to take up their property and follow him to the river Jordan, saying that he would divide the river by his command, and give them an easy passage, and thereby deceiving many[4]; or the Egyptian, who like-

[1] See Bishop Browne's Sermons on *The Messiah as Expected*, pp. 86, 87. Ebrard's *Gospel History*, p. 487.

[2] Comp. Matt. xvii. 22, 23 with the parallels.

[3] Luke xxiv. 21; John xx. 9. Comp. Milman's *Bampton Lectures*, p. 47.

[4] Josephus, *Antiq.* xx. 5, 1. See Westcott's *Introduction to the Gospel Narrative*, p. 125; Ebrard's *Gospel History*, 491.

wise persuaded the people that he was a prophet, and led thirty thousand from the wilderness to the Mount of Olives, promising to show them the walls of Jerusalem falling prostrate at his command[1]. Such, Josephus tells us, were but a few out of many who persuaded the people to indulge rash hopes, and led them forth into the wilderness under the idea that they should witness signs and prodigies, the precursors of their deliverance and restoration to independence[2]. 'Some of these men,' remarks Paley, 'it is probable might be impostors, who thought that an advantage was to be taken of the state of public opinion. Others, perhaps, were enthusiasts, whose imagination had been drawn to this particular object by the language and sentiments which prevailed around them. But, whether impostors or enthusiasts, they concurred in producing themselves in the character which their countrymen looked for, that is to say, as the restorers and deliverers of the nation, in that sense in which restoration and deliverance were expected by the Jews[3].'

Such, then, were the popular anticipations of the character and work of the Messiah at the era of the Advent. Neither in the early Jewish literature, nor in the writings of Hillel, of Philo, of Josephus, do we

[1] Joseph. *B. J.* II. 134, 135; *Antiq.* XX. 8. 6. These instances are a sufficient indication of the *kind* of miracles which the nation expected from the Messiah.

[2] 'In all of these we find not merely that they pretended to be *ordinary prophets*, but that they declare themselves to be filled with the Spirit of God, and to be commissioned in a miraculous way to secure for the people *political* freedom.' Ebrard, 491.

[3] Paley's *Evidences*, Part II. chap. II.

trace any expectation that the Messiah would sustain any relation to the Jewish sacrificial system; that the ancient ritual would disappear in consequence of His work[1]. And the fact that from the beginning the Jews were the most inveterate enemies with whom the Christians had to contend, that till this day they have rejected the claims of Christ to be the true Messiah, that His teaching offended the great men of His nation and its leaders, that by the course He took He disappointed His brethren and His disciples, and every hope and predilection of the people, must be a sufficient proof that the origin of the most extraordinary religious revolution the world has seen cannot be ascribed to the popular imagination of the age excited by Messianic hopes.

iii. But, thirdly, it has been maintained that this religious revolution had its origin *in a gradually developed mythology*. It is affirmed that after the death of the Institutor of this Rite, His disciples were filled with a vehement desire to reconcile His fate with the hopes respecting His person and work they had so fondly nurtured, and in some way to harmonise His sufferings and death with their Messianic ideas. Applying to His sufferings the numerous passages in the Old Testament in which men of God are described as suffering and put to death, they 'modified their pre-

[1] 'All who were zealous for the law, and they then included nine-tenths of the nation, were resolved to recognise no one as the true Messias unless he equalled and surpassed themselves in its observance with all its definitions, and in all its minutiæ, and with the whole "hedge" of interpretation around it.' Döllinger's *Jew and Gentile*, II. 331.

vious notions of the Messiah so as to suit such facts of His history as could not be denied,' and then, pressed by the objection that the true Messiah would work miracles, they ascribed miracles to Him suggested partly by well-known sayings of His, and partly by incidents of the Old Testament[1].

As to this extraordinary theory it may be observed first, that it raises ten times more difficulties than it explains. For, first of all, it requires of us to believe that, not at a period lost in a fabulous antiquity, but during one of which we know a great deal, and within historic times[2], illiterate men, as we know the early disciples were, could weave together such an extraordinary story and persuade many of their countrymen to accept it. It requires of us to receive this as the origin of the most extraordinary revolution the world has seen, though 'there is no known instance of a mythic history having grown up in such an age, under such circumstances, or with such rapidity[3] as is postulated in this case. The age was a historical age, being that of Dionysius, Diodorus, Livy, Velleius Paterculus,

1 See Ebrard's *Gospel History*, 475; Mill's *Pantheism*, p. 85.

2 'A period as historical as any that the ancient world presents to view; in which the transactions of every province within the limits of the late Macedonian and then Roman empire,—the barbarian, so termed, as well as the Grecian, and the acts of Herod among the number,—were the objects of research and careful narration, by natives of the soil as well as by strangers.' Mill's *Pantheism*, Part II. Sect. 2, p. 11; *Eclipse of Faith*, p. 210.

3 'For in A.D. 1 we find, by all remains of antiquity, that both Jews and Gentiles were reposing in the shadow of their ancient superstitions; and in A.D. 60, multitudes among *different* races had become the bigoted adherents of this novel *mythology!*' *Eclipse of Faith*, p. 210.

Plutarch, Valerius Maximus, and Tacitus; the country was one where written records were kept, and historical literature had long flourished; it produced, at the very time when the New Testament documents were being written, an historian of good repute, Josephus, whose narrative of the events of his own time is universally accepted as authentic and trustworthy. To suppose that a mythology could be formed in such an age and country, is to confuse the characteristics of the most opposite periods—to ascribe to a time of luxury, over-civilization, and decay, a phase of thought which only belongs to the rude vigour and early infancy of nations[1].'

But, secondly, if He who instituted this Rite did not fulfil the national expectations of the Messiah, if He disappointed every predilection and falsified every hope they had entertained, whence the anxiety to harmonise His fate with their previous ideas? Why did His disciples believe in Him any further? Why did they not go back to their homes and decline to trouble themselves with the matter, instead of courting certain danger by proclaiming Him in the very city where He had suffered a disgraceful end, as the Messiah and Hope of the nation? It is credible that a conviction that He was the Messiah may have attached them to Him *in the first instance* as disciples, but when His ignominious death gave the lie to that conviction, it is

[1] Rawlinson's *Bampton Lectures*, p. 223; *Cautions for the Times*, p. 513; Sherlock's *Trial of the Witnesses, Discourses*, Vol. IV. p. 360. 'The idea of men writing mythic histories between the time of Livy and Tacitus, and St Paul mistaking such for realities!' Dr Arnold, *Life*, II. p. 58.

simply incredible that a belief in Him should still have *survived.*

But, again, on this supposition, what conceivable motive can be assigned for their detaching themselves more and more from the religious observances of their forefathers, and in place of the ancient sacrificial ritual inculcating upon their followers the observance of a Rite which at every observance only proclaimed afresh *the disappointment of their former hopes?* With what object did they celebrate this Rite, and abstain from *imposing the celebration of any other?* They had joined in the sacrificial ritual of their forefathers for a clear and intelligible purpose[1]. Handed down from generation to generation, consecrated by the associations of the patriarchal age, and still more by the ordinances of their great Lawgiver, it had held a momentous place in their religious life, and they had ever been taught to believe that thereby they made good the imperfect consecration of themselves to God. But if He who instituted this Rite neither really wrought the miracles they ascribed to Him, nor satisfied their conceptions of the person and work of the Messiah, how came they to apply to Him the most august terms of a system consecrated by so many memories? how came they to see in His death the fulfilment of all previous sacrificial observances? What motive could have influenced them to isolate themselves from the religious views of the entire body of the nation, to forget their national zeal for the law and the traditions of the fathers, and, in

[1] See Butler's *Analogy*, Part II. chap. VI.

place of the varied and multiform ceremonies of ritual sanctioned by the command of God Himself, to receive themselves, and urge upon their followers, the celebration of a Rite so mysteriously simple as that of the Reception of Bread and Wine, in memory of an ignominious death upon the cross?

The force of this argument will be made apparent by a few additional considerations. Not only were they who first celebrated this Rite predisposed by every association of their previous history to maintain the existing sacrificial system, but, like that of the rest of their nation, their religion was an unbending Monotheism; they were opposed, with an intensity we can hardly conceive, to anything that even seemed to detract from the honour of Jehovah, the Lord of heaven and earth. Since the day that their forefathers returned from captivity, the Jewish people had not ceased to evince the utmost possible repugnance to idolatry in any form or shape. Oppressed and degraded as the nation was, the slightest tendency on the part of their rulers to enforce on them customs in the least degree savouring of idolatry was the signal for an outbreak of religious zeal which bore down everything before it. Herod the Great could not adorn his theatre with representations of the victories of Cæsar, or set up suits of armour in token of it, without incurring the charge of insulting the religious scruples of the people, and provoking a furious tumult[1]. The Roman governors

[1] Joseph. *Antiq.* IV. 8. 2. 'His attempt to place the Roman eagle on one of his new buildings produced a violent outbreak, and the at-

dared not introduce into the Holy City the military standards, which were deemed idolatrous, not only as bearing the symbol of the eagle, but also the image of Cæsar. Nay, when Pilate ventured to break through this rule, and introduced the obnoxious emblems during the night, his *prætorium* at Cæsarea was crowded for six days by numbers clamouring for their removal, upon whom threats of death were wasted, and who declared their perfect readiness to die rather than see their Law violated, so that the Procurator was utterly unable to withstand their importunity[1], and was obliged to remove the hated insignia. And later still the edict of Caligula, demanding that divine honour should be paid to himself, produced such a scene of tumult and bloodshed that even the Emperor was fain to yield[2].

But what were these infringements of the Law compared with the conduct of the disciples of the Institutor of this mysterious Rite? What was the unwitting caprice of a Herod, a Pilate, or a Caligula, compared with the strange and unprecedented teaching of this body of Jews, all zealous for the traditions of the fathers, and one a Pharisee and former pupil of the great Gamaliel? For the Rite which they observed, and which they inculcated on their followers,

tempt was not repeated. The extent to which the scruples of the Jews on this point were respected by the Roman governors, is shewn by the fact that no effigy of either God or emperor is found on the money coined by them in Judea before the war under Nero.' Ewald, *Geschichte*, V. 33, quoted in note on article Pontius Pilate in Smith's *Bib. Dictionary*.

[1] Joseph. *Antiq.* XVIII. 3, 1. 2; *B. J.* II. 9, § 2, 4.

[2] Milman's *History of the Jews*, II. 132, &c.

ascribed to the Institutor attributes before deemed to belong exclusively to Jehovah. The words, *Take, eat: this is My Body, broken for you; This Cup is the New Covenant in My Blood, which is shed for many for the remission of sins,* embodied in a palpable form the idea that the Being here commemorated could forgive sins, could exercise therefore the most awful and peculiar prerogative of Deity; 'for who,' to quote an objection of the teachers of the age, 'could forgive sins, but God only[1]?' Fearful of contamination with even the semblance of idolatry, shrinking with horror even from meat sold in the market that had been offered to idols, jealous of the least thing that threatened to derogate from the honour of their Law and the majesty of their God, they yet celebrated a Rite which, while it commemorated the death of One who yielded up His life upon the cross, ascribed to Him those attributes which they had been taught from their earliest years belonged only to God. Bread which before, whether at a solemn Paschal Feast, or at a Passover-Eve service, or at an ordinary meal[2], the head of the family

[1] Mk ii. 7. 'The fact that men strictly trained in Judaism, like St Paul, give in their writings to Christ such high Divine predicates, which stand in direct contradiction with Jewish monotheism, remains inexplicable, unless we presume a total and overmastering change of their religious views.' Dorner's *Person of Christ*, Vol. I. p. 47. E. T.

[2] The point here indicated will be more fully handled below; meanwhile it will be sufficient to refer in proof to Buxtorf's *Synagoga;* to the translation of the Mishna by Raphall, pp. 7, 8; Godwyn's *Moses and Aaron;* Stuckius *de Conviviis;* Freeman's *Principles of Divine Service*, pp. 294, 5, &c.; and the *Book of Religion, Ceremonies, and Prayers of the Jews*, by Gamaliel Ben Pedahzur, London, 1738.

had broken, distributed, and eaten in remembrance of the One Supreme Jehovah, 'who had created the fruit of the ground,' they now broke, distributed, and ate in remembrance of One who had died upon 'the accursed tree!' The cup of wine which on every similar occasion they had drunk with special remembrance of the Lord their God 'who created the fruit of the vine,' they now drank in memory of One whom, 'a very scorn of men,' and 'an outcast from the people,' they had seen suspended between two thieves; nay, they drank it as symbolizing the blood ratifying a new Covenant, and shed not for them only, but—marvellous contrast to the exclusiveness of Judaism!—for 'many,' for the whole world, for 'the remission of sins!' And this they did, though the whole genius of Judaism was utterly opposed to human sacrifices; though their past history suggested nothing analogous to this Rite, for, herein differing from Gentile nations, they had feasts indeed in 'memory of some great and rare passage of Divine Providence,' but no single feast in honour of any particular person, however high, however holy, Abraham, or Moses, or David[1]! What powerful and constraining motive can have induced plain

[1] 'We find among the Greeks their *Αἰάκεια* in honour of Æacus, their *Αἰάντεια* in honour of Ajax, and in later times their *Ἀντιγόνεια*, and such like, in remembrance of the merits of such persons, and how highly they deserved of the places where their feasts were celebrated. In like sort the Jews had their feasts in memory of some great and rare passage of Divine Providence, *though not of any particular persons, lest they should be tempted to worship them as their Saviours, according as the custom of the heathen was.*' Patrick's *Mensa Mystica*, *Works*, I. 98, Ed. 1858.

unsophisticated men to celebrate themselves, and to inculcate on others, the celebration of a Rite so strange and utterly unprecedented? Whence this extraordinary change of feeling towards the Law and the Ritual of their fathers, consecrated by a thousand memories, hallowed by the approval of God Himself? Whence, almost at the same period, a readiness to rise in frenzied rebellion against the introduction into the Holy City of the standards and image of the Emperor, and a readiness to celebrate an ordinance which claimed for a crucified Man the incommunicable attributes of Deity? And, still more, how comes it to pass that when the followers of the Institutor of this Rite carry it with them into other lands, and proclaim the story it 'shews forth,' the same extraordinary change of feeling respecting the ancient sacrificial ritual is found operating in heathen nations, so that, to quote a single instance out of many that might be adduced, a Roman governor of Pontus and Bithynia could complain to the Emperor Trajan, that, in consequence of the spread of the tenets first preached by these *plain unsophisticated men*, the temples of the gods were forsaken, the sacred solemnities intermitted, and the *victims found few purchasers*[1]?

[1] See C. Plin. Trajano Imp. Lib. x. Ep. xcvii. 'No evidence remains,' remarks Paley, 'by which it can be proved that the Christians were more numerous in Pontus and Bithynia than in other parts of the Roman Empire; nor has any reason been offered to show why they should be so. Christianity did not begin in these countries, nor near them. I do not know, therefore, that we ought to confine the description in Pliny's letter to the state of Christianity in those provinces, even if no other account of the same subject had come down to us.' *Evidences*, Part II. chap. 9.

From these considerations, then, it is apparent that, if the Institutor of this Rite, while He claimed to be the Messiah, passed away without doing anything more than disappoint every Messianic hope and predilection, no conceivable reason can be assigned for their believing in Him at all after His death; for their voluntarily exposing themselves to labours, dangers and sufferings, as believers in Him; for the unprecedented position, which, considering they were Jews, they take up in reference to the Mosaic law; for their detaching themselves more and more from the ancient sacrificial ritual, while they *intensified the feeling of guilt and individual shortcoming, of which all sacrifice was the expression;* for their receiving and celebrating a Rite not only utterly alien to any similar institution of Judaism, not only recalling at each celebration the disappointment of their former Messianic hopes, but ascribing to Him whose death was therein symbolized the incommunicable prerogative of Deity—the remission of sins; for their being able, on proclaiming the story of His life and death in other lands, to produce *instinctively, and not by force or violence,* an effect on the heathen sacrificial ritual which has lasted from that day to this, and has obliterated from the recollections of successive generations a form of religious worship once universal throughout the world.

CHAPTER IV.

EXAMINATION OF THE GOSPEL NARRATIVE.

> *'Η τροφὴ αὕτη καλεῖται παρ' ἡμῖν Εὐχαριστία· ἧς οὐδενὶ ἄλλῳ μετασχεῖν ἐξόν ἐστιν, ἢ τῷ πιστεύοντι ἀληθῆ εἶναι τὰ δεδιδαγμένα ὑφ' ἡμῶν.*
>
> JUSTIN MARTYR.

THESE theories being utterly insufficient to account for the reception of this Rite, or to explain the extraordinary effect upon the ancient Jewish and Gentile sacrificial customs which has instinctively accompanied its reception, we turn to the Gospel Narrative, and proceed to enquire whether it can supply that adequate and consistent explanation which we are seeking.

And before actually doing so, let us briefly recapitulate the chief points which require explanation.

From the only account of the origin of this Rite which has come down to us, we learn that its Institutor enjoined its celebration upon His followers *before His death.*

That death—the ignominious death of the malefactor and the slave—which the concurrent testimony of Christian and heathen writers declares that He underwent, was the culminating point of the disappointment His whole life had been to the hopes, the anticipations, the predilections of His disciples, His relatives and His nation.

His first disciples lived in a sacrificial age, and had been trained in sacrificial habits from their earliest years; in common with the rest of their nation they were attached, with a devotion we can hardly realize, to their ancestral faith, to its ordinances, its ceremonial, and its traditions; they were intensely jealous of any even the least interference with their religion, and were ready to die rather than see the least of its peculiar institutions disregarded.

And yet they did not scruple to proclaim the fulfilment of all the ordinances and ceremonies of their ancient faith in the death of their Master; though they had been brought up under a rigid monotheism they from the first transferred to Him the attributes of the one true God; wherever they went they succeeded in persuading men to accept and celebrate a Rite which commemorated His death; and wherever this Rite has been accepted the ancient sacrificial ritual has entirely disappeared.

These are facts of history.

i. Now it is inconceivable that they could have done this, and at the same time proclaimed the worthlessness of the prevailing sacrificial ritual, *unless the death commemorated in the Eucharist could be regarded not only as a propitiatory sacrifice, but one which, in a far higher and more efficacious degree than they had ever known before, realized to them that pardon of sin, and that restoration to the Divine favour which they had ever believed to be in some mysterious way secured to them by the offering of the ancient sacrifices.* We repeat *in a far higher and more efficacious degree*[1]. For we do not find this Rite ever put on equality with other sacrificial rites however costly or splendid; the latter are uniformly and unhesitatingly spoken of as 'done away' and 'fulfilled.'

ii. To be able to speak of the death therein 'shewn forth' as possessing this surpassing efficacy, it is clear that *the first observers of this Rite must have had some indubitable proof of the acceptance of the Sacrifice it symbolized.* They must have been able to appeal to some clear attestation of its acceptance as a sacrifice for sin. On a point of this kind imagination was powerless. They must have been able to give some satisfactory account of the matter, before they could persuade multitudes *of all nations* to lay aside their ancient sacrifices, and adopt a Rite so novel and unprecedented[2].

[1] 'In writings addressed to those whose religious system was entirely based upon a doctrine of atonement, the point to be shewn was, not that *an* atonement for sin was necessary, but *that the Atonement itself*, of which intelligent Jews must see that the blood of lambs and he-goats could only be a type and a shadow, was to be *found in its full substance and reality in the Cross of Jesus Christ.*' Cowie's *Hulsean Lectures* for 1855, p. 24.

[2] 'The fact of a Christian Church being *formed at all*, notwithstanding the shock which the idea of a crucified Messiah must necessarily have given to the mind of every Israelite of that day, can only be explained on the assumption of the Divinity of Christ and the historical reality of His Resurrection.' Ebrard's *Gospel History*, 447. 'We shall, therefore, not say too much if we designate the Supper the climax of the

iii. And, further, when we look at the narrative of the Institution of this Rite as it has come down to us, we cannot but be struck with its remarkable brevity and conciseness. Considering all that it was designed to import, considering its utterly unprecedented character as a Jewish institution, considering the shock which the idea of commemorating the death of a crucified Messiah must necessarily have given to the mind of every Israelite of that day, it is brief to a degree perfectly astonishing. This brevity has been noticed[1] as a proof of the genuineness of the narrative. Had the account been forged, it is said, or had it been introduced in a later age, it would certainly have been more full and more formal. This brevity is further worthy of note as proving that the first disciples must have been *prepared for the contemplation of the death of their Master* in the light of a sacrifice, otherwise it is unaccountable that, in spite of its unprecedented character, we find nowhere in the Epistles any *long, laboured, and special justification* of the use of this Rite in place of the ancient sacrificial ritual.

One main object, then, of our review of the Gospel Narrative will be to shew that the minds of the first disciples were *prepared* by their Master for this view of His death. We shall try to group together all the passages which bear upon this subject, and to shew

ancient Christian worship, in which the congregation celebrated its reconciliation with God in Christ, the Mediator between God and men; and find in its uninterrupted celebration *the first proof of the stedfast faith of the Church in the divine nature of Christ.*' Dorner, I. 168. E. T.

[1] Paley's *Evidences.*

how naturally and consistently they conspire together towards this point, and are at the same time replete with 'coincidences which, if ingenuity had been subtle enough to fabricate, that same ingenuity would have been too sagacious to conceal so deep, and which are too numerous and striking to be the effect of accident[1].' *From the beginning to the end, and not in consequence of any after-thought or change of plan,* we shall see that the idea of the Saviour's death was ever set forth as a sacrifice for sin; in the institution of the Lord's Supper we shall trace the culminating point of all previous revelations on this subject; and in the fact of the Resurrection we shall see the strongest *proof* of the Divinity of the Saviour, and at the same time of the acceptance of His death as an atonement for the sins of the whole world.

Now it cannot be denied that the Saviour's public ministry divides itself into two main parts, that the Baptism inaugurates the one, the Transfiguration the other[2]. During the former period His actions and teaching 'are a commentary on the text that Jesus is the Christ of God.' He gathers to Him His disciples, lays down the laws of His kingdom, performs His great redemptive works, the 'signs' of His Divine mission; then, not till then, does He begin to intimate clearly and unmistakeably that He must 'suffer many things.'

But on a somewhat closer examination we shall find

[1] *Eclipse of Faith*, p. 312.

[2] Archbp. Thomson's *Bampton Lectures*, p. 96.

that *at sundry times* and *in divers manners*[1] intimations are given *from the very beginning* of the End which awaited Him; that it is *the* point from first to last to which the Gospel Narrative tends as the fore-appointed source of the blessings which the Saviour came to bestow upon mankind.

Let us, then, first consider the intimations made during the period intervening between the Saviour's birth and His visit to Jerusalem at the first Passover of His public ministry.

And here the first point which claims our attention is the fact that the explanation given by the angel before His birth of His name, JESUS, assumes, from the very commencement as the main purpose of His entrance into the world, *a definite connection with that which lies at the root of all sacrifice, Jewish or Gentile, namely, Sin, or a state of alienation from God.*

The Name, which is *above every name,* was twice, as we know, announced before His birth. On the first occasion to the Virgin, on the second in a dream to Joseph. To the Virgin the angel said, *Fear not, Mary; for thou hast found favour with God, and behold thou shalt conceive in thy womb, and shalt bring forth a Son, and thou shalt call His name JESUS. He shall be great, and shall be called the Son of the Highest, and the Lord God shall give Him the throne of His father David, and He shall reign over the house of Jacob for ever, and of His kingdom there shall be no end*[2]. But when the same name was announced to Joseph, 'per-

[1] Heb. i. 1. [2] Lk. i. 30—33.

chance the aged Joseph[1],' whose spiritual faculties had perhaps long been refined and purified to realise the deepest needs of men, it was surrounded with a very different train of associations. *Fear not,* said the Angel to him, *to take unto thee Mary thy wife: for that which is conceived in her is of the Holy Ghost, and she shall bring forth a Son, and thou shalt call His name JESUS: for He shall save His people from their sins*[2]. He announced to him the birth not of any mere redresser of His country's wrongs, not of any moral teacher, not of any Prophet, not of any King, but of a Saviour, of a *Deliverer from sin.* The same name Jesus, as applied to the successor of Moses and conqueror of Palestine[3], had a peculiar significance. He who was first Hoshea, '*salvation,*' and afterwards Jehoshua, or Joshua, '*God's-salvation,*' was to deliver Israel from literal living enemies, the Canaanites. The same name, as now applied to the true Joshua, equally suggests a deliverance to be effected, *He shall deliver His people from their sins.*

Now when we reflect on the position in the Gospel Narrative which this title and its explanation occupy, we see at once that it can never be consistently alleged

[1] See Ellicott's *Hulsean Lectures*, p. 56.

[2] Matt. i. 21. Ἐνταῦθα τὸ παράδοξον ἐνδείκνυται. Οὐ γὰρ πολέμων αἰσθητῶν, οὐδὲ βαρβάρων, ἀλλ' ὃ πολλῷ τούτων μεῖζον ἦν, ἁμαρτημάτων ἀπαλλαγὴν εὐαγγελίζεται· ὃ μηδενί ποτε ἔμπροσθεν ἐγένετο δυνατόν. S. Chrysost. *in loc.*

[3] For some striking remarks on the associations connected with the name Joshua, see Pearson *on the Creed*, Art. II.; also Dean Stanley's *Jewish Church*, p. 227.

either that (1) any connection, which may afterwards be more prominently developed, between the life and work of the Saviour and man's sense of sin, or (2) that any relation that may be discerned between His death and the existing sacrificial system, is an *afterthought.* Coming in where these words do, uttered at a time when the heart of the nation was set upon the realization of temporal glories as the result of the coming of the Messiah, and was convinced of its spiritual superiority to all other nations, they prove[1] that no one could have spoken them, who believed the popular Messianic idea to be the true one, and that they could not have proceeded from the popular imagination excited by Messianic hopes.

Bearing in mind this early intimation of the spiritual nature of the Saviour's work, let us pass on. *Made of a woman, born under the law*[2], at the legal period the Holy Child underwent the Jewish ceremony of circumcision, and was afterwards presented by His parents in the Temple[3]. At the moment that they were entering the sacred precincts, they were met by the aged Symeon, who had long *been waiting for the consolation of Israel,* and to whom it had been revealed that he should not taste of death till he had seen the

[1] 'Coming in where these words do, they outweigh a thousand cavils against the historical reality of the narration. If I mistake not, this announcement reaches further into the deliverance to be wrought by Jesus, than anything mentioned by the Evangelist subsequently.' Dean Alford on S. Matt. i. 21.

[2] Gal. iv. 4.

[3] S. Lk. ii. 22—38.

Messiah. No sooner, then, did he behold the Child than he saw that the long-promised hour was come. He took Him up in his arms, and blessed God, that his eyes had been *permitted to see His Salvation, the Light to lighten the Gentiles, and the Glory of His people Israel*[1]. Then while Joseph and Mary were marvelling at his words, he blessed them also, and addressing the Virgin-Mother[2], said, *Behold, this Child is set* (*or appointed*) *for the fall and rising again of many in Israel, and for a sign that shall be spoken against; yea, a sword shall pierce through thy own soul also, that the thoughts of many hearts may be revealed.* A sword shall pierce through thy own soul also! Interpret these mysterious words how we will, we cannot deny that there is already a dark shadow flung upon the Virgin's joy, a presentiment of some terrible trial to come upon her. The aged Seer, already on the verge of the eternal world, foresees in store for her no gilded pageants, no worldly pomp, no seat on the right hand or on the left in a glorious kingdom, such as would befit the mother of the Messiah whom the nation expected. Her child is destined to be a *stone of stumbling and a rock of offence to some,* to others a source of exaltation, while for herself—*a sword is to pierce through her heart.* How strangely is the light and shadow already blended! How entirely do these presentiments of a chequered future clash with all ideas of the person and work of the Messiah then agitating the popular imagination,

[1] Lk. ii. 32.

[2] καὶ εἶπε πρὸς Μαριὰμ τὴν μητέρα αὐτοῦ, Luke ii. 34.

but how perfectly they coincide with the angelic announcement of a *Deliverer of His people from Sin!*

Between the Presentation in the Temple, and the commencement of the Saviour's public ministry there is an interval of thirty years. These years, as we cannot but have often remarked, are well-nigh a blank to us. Besides the visit of the Magi to Jerusalem, the cruel decree of Herod, the consequent flight into Egypt, the return of Joseph and Mary into the land of Galilee, their residence at Nazareth, and the visit to the Temple when the Saviour was twelve years of age, there is not a fact recorded respecting this long interval. The Evangelists shroud it in a complete silence[1]. With staid self-constraint, utterly unlike the spirit of sign-seeking characteristic of their age, they dim not the lustre of their pages with any of those premature proofs of superhuman power which the Apocryphal Gospels[2] love to record. With a few simple and artless touches they portray a picture which has no parallel in the world, the picture of a spotless and celestial childhood ripening into a perfect manhood[3]. *He went down with His parents to Nazareth,*

[1] On this reverent silence as contrasted with the Apocryphal Gospels see Ellicott's *Lectures*, p. 97; Birks' *Bible and Modern Thought*, p. 397.

[2] See Tischendorf's *Evangelia Apocrypha*.

[3] Lk. ii. 51. 'The idea of sinlessness was by no means so common an idea, that all that was necessary to lead men like the Apostles to apply it to Christ was an accident or some insufficient occasion. Quite the contrary: this idea was never thought of, nor had it entered into the heart of man to conceive it, until it appeared not as an idea merely, but as a reality in the life of Jesus of Nazareth. Even now to

to Nazareth, which then enjoyed a reputation so low that the question was put as though it contained its own answer, not by a proud Jew of the South, but by a native of Galilee, *Can any good thing come out of Nazareth*[1]*?* and there He grew *in wisdom and stature, and in favour with God and man*[2].

And now the period of silence and seclusion is over. Jerusalem, Judea, and all the country round about Jordan has been startled by the sudden appearance of a strange and wondrous Preacher, recalling in dress, and garb, and gesture, the expected forerunner of the Messiah, the great Elijah. In striking congruity with the spiritual nature of the Saviour's work, the son of Zacharias proclaims that the kingdom of heaven is at hand, that one was to come after him of surpassing dignity, that he was unworthy to unloose even the latchet of his shoe, but he dwells on no *temporal glories* to be vouchsafed to the nation. *Repentance*, deep and real, he demands of all that would receive baptism at his hands, and warns them against the idea that mere descent from Abraham would qualify any for admission into the kingdom of the Messiah. And at length when these announcements, so unlike any of the popular conceptions of the Messiah's coming, have prepared hearts

believe in the realizing of the idea of sinlessness in an individual, is not so very easy a thing for human nature in its present state. Men are not in general much addicted to the weakness of believing too easily in the existence of purity of heart and true greatness: it is a fact, that they are only too prone to doubt them when they really exist.' Ullmann's *Sinlessness of Jesus*, p. 91.

[1] Jn. i. 46.

[2] Lk. ii. 52.

to receive Him, the Saviour leaves the seclusion of the Galilean village, and moves southward to the valley of the Jordan. At the hands of His Forerunner He receives the rite of Baptism, and the first of the three voices from heaven is heard attesting His Divine mission, and declaring Him to be in very deed the *Son of God, in whom the Father is well pleased*[1]. And now that He has been inaugurated to His work, what is the first event of His ministry? Borne by the motions of the Spirit into the wilderness[2], He enters into a conflict with the great Adversary of His kingdom, and of the race He came to save. Into the details of this conflict we are not concerned to enter now. The single point to which we would invite attention is the singular congruity of this conflict with the avowed purport of the Saviour's mission, a congruity which at once commends it to our minds, and which transcends all powers of. imagination, or preconcerted imposition.

But when the Forty Days of the mysterious Temptation were ended, the Saviour again approached the Jordan's banks, and the scene of His Baptism. The Baptist was still there; he was still delivering his message, and exhorting the multitudes to repentance. The day before he had received a formal deputation from the ruling parties at Jerusalem to ask him who he was, and why he baptized[3]. To them he had spoken plainly and decisively. He had assured them he was neither the Messiah, nor Elias, nor the Prophet, but

[1] Matt. iii. 13; Mk. i. 11; Lk. iv. 22.

[2] Matt. iv. 1, and the parallels.

[3] Jn. i. 21.

simply the *Voice of one crying in the wilderness, Make straight the way of the Lord*[1]. But now again[2] he saw the lowly One of Nazareth drawing near on His way, we may believe, to Galilee, and no sooner did he behold Him approaching than he exclaimed, *Behold the Lamb of God, that taketh away*[3] *the sin of the world;* he declared that this was He who was to come *after him*, but who was originally *before him*[4], this was He on whom he had seen the Spirit descending and abiding[5], this was He that was to baptize with the Holy Ghost[6], this was the *Son of God*[7]. Nor was it once only that this mysterious title of *the Lamb of God* fell from his lips. On the very day[8] after, in the hearing of two of his disciples[9], fixing his eye on Jesus as he walked, he said, *Behold the Lamb of God;* and such was the effect upon his hearers, that, drawn as it were by a powerful magnet, they left the Baptist and *followed Jesus.*

Now the title here given by the Baptist to the Saviour, whether we consider the time or the occasion

[1] Jn. i. 23.
[2] Jn. i. 29.
[3] Jn. i. 29.
[4] Jn. i. 30.
[5] Jn. i. 32.
[6] Jn. i. 33.
[7] Jn. i. 34.
[8] Τῇ ἐπαύριον. Jn. i. 35.
[9] Ἐμβλέψας (*Aspectus efficax*, Bengel) τῷ Ἰησοῦ περιπατοῦντι. John i. 36. Διὰ τοῦτο λοιπὸν ἀναγκάζεται τὰ αὐτὰ λέγειν πάλιν, καθάπερ τινὰ σκληρὰν καὶ ἀνένδοτον γῆν τῇ νεώσει μαλάττων, καὶ τῷ λόγῳ οἱόν τινι ἀρότρῳ πεπιλημένην ἀνεγείρων τὴν διανοίαν, ὥστε εἰς τὸ βάθος τὰ σπέρματα καταβαλεῖν. Διὰ δὴ τοῦτο οὐδὲ μακρὸν ποιεῖ τὸν λόγον, ὅτι ἓν μόνον ἐσπούδαζε, προσαγαγεῖν αὐτοὺς καὶ κολλῆσαι τῷ Χριστῷ. Ἤδει γὰρ ὅτι τοῦτο καταδεξάμενοι καὶ πεισθέντες, οὐ δεήσονται τοῦ μαρτυρήσοντος αὐτῷ λοιπόν. S. Chrysost. *in Joann.* Hom. XVIII.

of its bestowal, is deserving of much attention. Commentators, indeed, have often debated what may have been the precise train of thought which suggested it. Some have imagined that a flock of lambs may have been passing on their way to the coming Passover[1] at Jerusalem. Others have seen in it an allusion to the lamb of the morning and evening sacrifice at the Temple. Others, with far greater probability, have referred it to that wonderful chapter in the prophet Isaiah[2], which afterwards so powerfully arrested the attention of the Ethiopian eunuch[3]. But whatever may have been the precise line of thought which suggested the image, whether the reference be special or comprehensive[4], the point deserving of notice, is that the work of the Messiah is *already viewed in connection with the ancient sacrificial system*, the idea of a perfect Antitype of all the typical lambs of the ancient ritual has already dawned, and sacrificial terms begin, in the hearing of Apostles[5], to associate themselves with His

[1] Jn. ii. 13. Ἐγγὺς ἦν τὸ πάσχα τῶν Ἰουδαίων. Milman's *History of Christianity*, Vol. I. p. 158. See Alford on S. John i. 22, and his *Hulsean Lectures* for 1841.

[2] Isaiah liii. 7. See Tholuck *on S. John*, p. 84, E. T. Ἀμνὸν δὲ αὐτὸν καλεῖ, τῆς προφητείας ἀναμιμνήσκων Ἰουδαίους τῆς Ἡσαΐου, καὶ τῆς σκιᾶς τῆς κατὰ τὸν Μωϋσέα. S. Chrysost. *in Joann.* Hom. XVII.

[3] Acts viii. 30—34.

[4] See Archbp. Trench's *Five Sermons before the University of Cambridge*, p. 23, Ed. 1857.

[5] Jn. i. 35, S. Andrew, and, according to almost universal belief, S. John. It is not a little striking that it is S. John who transfigures this title of the Lamb of God in the majestic language of the Apocalypse (the term *ἀρνίον* as applied to Christ occurs 29 times in the Revelation), and that S. Peter, whom his brother Andrew first 'found' and 'brought

person and office. And who is it that thus associates them? Is it some Levite, whose office obliges him from day to day to wait upon the priests at the altar, and to witness the slaying of 'bulls and goats'? Is it the high-priest of the nation, whose thoughts it may be said were merely borrowed from the mechanical functions of his office? On the contrary, it is one who was pre-eminently a moral teacher and reformer, who, though the son of a priest, yet never in his recorded addresses to the people who flocked to his baptism, dwells on the ritual ordinances of the Law, or bids them observe days and seasons, and multiply sacrifices. Real, genuine repentance, *distrust in the mere possession of privileges*[1], this was John's message to the world. On the people, eagerly excited by the anticipation of the Messiah's Advent, he inculcates the plain practical duty of mutual charity[2]; on the hated tax-gatherers, of honesty[3]; and on the rough and often brutal soldiers, of mercy and contentment[4]. His language is that of the sternest of the Old Testament Prophets, the language of one as far removed from merely ritual and ceremonial ideas as was ever his great prototype Elijah. No man was more intensely real and practical than the Baptist. From the midst of a corrupt and decaying world he had fled into the deserts, and lived the life of the Nazarite, a life of abstinence and austerity. In

to Jesus,' (Jn. i. 41), saying, We have 'found the Messias,' alone of the Apostles speaks of the Christian as redeemed by the precious blood of Christ, as *of a lamb without blemish and without spot*, 1 Pet. i. 19.

[1] Lk. iii. 8. [2] Lk. iii. 11. [3] Lk. iii. 13. [4] Lk. iii. 14.

solitude and silence he had communed with his God, had weighed the things of time and sense in the balances of heaven, and had come forth to demand a radical reformation of his generation, if they would be a people prepared for the Messiah. But no moral Teacher greater than himself does he announce to his disciples, no mere Redresser of the nation's wrongs, no Prophet only like unto Moses, no King like unto David, but One who, though so infinitely his superior that he was not worthy to stoop down and unloose His sandal, though attested as the *Son of God* by a Voice from heaven, was yet the LAMB, given by God, or sent by God, or well-pleasing to God, who was *to take away the sin of the world.* Whatever was the precise import attached to the title by those who heard it and whom it attracted to the Saviour's Person, there is a remarkable congruity between it and the angelic announcement on the world's first Christmas morn of the birth of a *Saviour*[1]—the intimation to Joseph of the spiritual nature of the work of the *Deliverer from sin,* and the mysterious prophetic glance of the aged Simeon[2]. Is it likely that an *idealist* would have put the intimation of the *sacrificial* nature of the Saviour's work into the mouth of a *moral teacher* like the Baptist[3]? Is it

[1] Comp. 'The glad tidings for you and *for all people*' (Luke ii. 10) with the 'sin *of the world*' in John i. 29. 'Singularis numerus, cum articulo, summa vi, una pestis quæ totum corripuit. Peccatum et mundus æque late patent.' Bengel.

[2] Tholuck *on S. John*, p. 85, E. T.

[3] The force of the Baptist's words, considering the time when they were uttered, is strongly felt by rationalistic writers. 'Strauss, Weisse,

credible that the harmony of several testimonies to one idea, and that utterly opposed to the prevailing popular belief, can have been the result of a gradual accretion of myths?

Very shortly after this momentous declaration of the Baptist, the Saviour left the region where he was baptizing, and retired into Galilee. There, on the occasion of the marriage-feast at Cana, He displayed for the first time His miraculous power, and confirmed the faith of the little band of disciples who had already attached themselves to Him, numbering, besides Andrew and John, Simon Peter, Philip, and Nathanael. At the conclusion of the feast, with His mother, His brethren, and His newly-gathered followers, He went down to Capernaum. There, however, His stay was of no long duration[1]. The Passover *was nigh at hand*[2], the pilgrim-companies were already forming to go up to the Holy City, and thither with His disciples, after a short interval, He bent His steps. Before entering, however, on the deeply important revelations respecting His person and work made at this the first Passover of

and Bruno Bauer declare it *impossible* that John the Baptist should know anything of the pre-existence of Jesus, and of his *vicarious sufferings*. Galler, Paulus, and Hug endeavour to soften down the meaning of the words αἴρειν τὴν ἁμαρτίαν. Hoffmann tries to explain the matter psychologically as a sudden flash of light. But apart from the fact of the connection of the Baptist with the mother of our Lord,...the fact that he was a prophet and enlightened by the Lord, is sufficient to set all such questions at rest, as "how can he have obtained a foresight of the sufferings of Jesus?" The difficulty is not *historical*, but purely *dogmatical*.' Ebrard's *Gospel History*, p. 209; Tholuck *on S. John*, p. 85.

[1] Οὐ πολλὰς ἡμέρας, Jn. ii. 12.

[2] Jn. ii. 13.

His public ministry, we would make a few remarks on a point which has given rise to certain objections. We have listened to the words of Angels, we have heard the intimation given to Joseph, the prophetic utterance of Simeon, the last testimony of the Baptist; we are now about to listen to the WORD Himself, to hear from His own gracious lips of the purport and object of His coming into the world.

Now believing that His Advent into the world was the Pole-star of the prophecies and revelations of the Old Testament, it will be worth while to look back for a moment and observe what constituted one of their most characteristic features, namely their *gradual and progressive development.* In this respect they are in complete accord with the Divine operations in the natural world; as in nature there is first the blade, then the ear, and then the full corn in the ear; first the dawn, then the morning, and then the perfect day; first the child, then the youth, and then the man; so is it in the gradual unfolding of the person and work of man's Redeemer. The first promise of a Saviour[1] did, perhaps, little more than *assure* man of an interposition in his behalf, and neither informed him whether the promised conqueror of his seducer should be one or many, the collective race or a single deliverer. But of a deliverance he *was* assured[2], and from the time it was first given this promise of ultimate de-

[1] Gen. iii. 15. See Kurtz *on the Old Covenant*, Vol. I. p. 79, E. T. See Sherlock *on the Prophecies*, Disc. III. p. 65, Ed. 1732.

[2] See Davison *on Prophecy*, p. 55.

liverance becomes the goal of Sacred History, the one centre towards which it persistently gravitates. Each crisis in the world's history brings it within narrower limits, and illustrates it with fresh details. Through one of the sons of Noah[1] the promise is limited to a particular race; through the Call of Abraham[2], to a particular nation; through Judah, to a particular tribe[3]. With the Mosaic period the *personality* of the Redeemer begins to be more distinctly developed, and Israel is taught to look forward to a great Prophet[4]. With the establishment of David's kingdom, the promise is not only still further narrowed to a single family, but the idea of a king[5] is associated with the person of the destined Deliverer. The later and mournful history, however, of the kingdom serves to correct the national hopes, the captivity refines and purifies the Messianic idea, and the 'Son of David' gives place in the writings of Daniel to the 'Son of Man[6].' Concurrently with the altering fortunes of the nation, another voice begins to be heard in the temple of prophecy, not jubilant and glad, telling of triumph and glory, of the subjugation of nations, and the setting up of an everlasting throne, but subdued and mournful, whispering of suffering and rejection, of the coming of

[1] Gen. ix. 26.

[2] Gen. xii. 1—3.

[3] Gen. xlix. 10. See Westcott on the Jewish Doctrine of Messiah, *Introd. to N. T.* p. 86.

[4] Deut. xviii. 15—18. See Davison, p. 110; Kurtz *on the Old Covenant*, Vol. II.

[5] 2 Sam. vii. 12—17. Comp. Psalm lxxxix; Davison, 142.

[6] Dan. vii. 13. Westcott, p. 87; Article '*Son of Man*,' in Smith's *Dictionary of the Bible*, III. 1359; *Aids to Faith*, p. 119.

a man of sorrow and acquainted with grief[1], of His *being wounded for transgressions and bruised for iniquities, of Messiah being cut off*[2], *but not for Himself,* of His *bearing the sin of many,* of His *being numbered with the transgressors.* That these later prophecies were misunderstood by the Jews, or rather that they hid their faces from them, is indisputable. But regarding them as included within their Scriptures, we cannot fail to observe how gradually the idea of a suffering Messiah was permitted to dawn upon the nation. It may be said that it was wrapped up and included in the first promises that irradiated the exile from Eden, for the serpent was *to bruise the heel* of man's Deliverer. But how could the Jewish nation have been educated at all to become, as they did, 'the people of the future'? how could they have been kept in the attitude of expectation, not pining, like the heathen world, over the departed glories of a former golden age, but looking for 'one to come,' if they had been told, 'the object of all your hopes, He in whom ye trust, shall suffer and shall die'? Abrupt announcements like these are not the methods of teaching employed by Him who knoweth whereof 'man is made,' who mercifully hides from him the future of his life, and only when he can 'bear it' reveals its sorrow or its joy.

[1] Isaiah liii. Comp. vii. 14; ix. 6; xl. 1, 12; xlii. 1, 4; xlix. 5, 7; lii; liv. On the reference of Isa. liii. to the Messiah even in the Modern Jewish Service-Books, see *Aids to Faith,* p. 127.

[2] Dan. ix. 26.

Such a gradual revelation, then, of the object of the coming of the Messiah being one of the characteristic features of the prophecies of the Old Testament, we shall be prepared for the same characteristics in the New; and it will not surprise us if we do not find the Saviour setting forth at the outset of His ministry, *fully* and *clearly* and in set terms, a connection between His work and the ancient sacrificial system. We shall not complain if, at this early period, even when He predicts His death, 'He does not put forward with equal clearness its atoning virtue,' as some have complained. Considering what human nature is everywhere, considering the extreme difficulty of gaining a lodgment for the idea of a suffering Messiah at all in such an age as that of the Advent, we shall be prepared for its gradual revelation, and shall certainly not be tempted to impute such a *gradual* revelation to an afterthought[1], to disappointment, or to other irreverent motives, which some have not scrupled to impute to the Holy One. We shall see in such a course of gradual instruction in unpalatable truths what we should expect from a wise human teacher, how much more from Him Who, as we have seen, thus 'spake by the Prophets' of the Old Testament!

[1] See the quotation in Thomson's *Bampton Lectures*, from De Wette, *de Morte Christi expiatoria*, and Ullmann *on the Sinlessness of Jesus*, p. 151, notes.

CHAPTER V.

THE EARLY PUBLIC MINISTRY.

Ἔτι πολλὰ ἔχω λέγειν ὑμῖν, ἀλλ' οὐ δύνασθε βαστάζειν ἄρτι.
S. JOHN xvi. 12.

THE Passover, then, was nigh at hand, and Jesus went up to Jerusalem[1]. Year by year, S. Luke intimates, He had been wont to go thither with His parents, and at this same Festival eighteen years before He had astonished the Jewish doctors by 'His understanding and answers[2].' He was now in the prime of life, and His public ministry had begun. Knowing what was to take place at this Festival two years afterwards, we observe His actions on this occasion with the utmost interest, and listen to His words with the deepest attention. We try to realise the scene which Jerusalem presented at this time; the multitudes of Jews and proselytes from all quarters of the world that had come up to celebrate the Feast; the hills around the Holy City whitened with countless flocks of lambs

[1] Jn. ii. 13.

[2] Lk. ii. 47.

and kids[1]; and then we think of HIM, already pointed out as the 'Lamb of God,' appearing in the midst of this moving scene[2], and celebrating the Festival with the pilgrim-company from Galilee.

We have no record, indeed, of any actual participation in a Paschal Supper on this occasion, but we have the record of a deeply momentous circumstance which took place during the festival. Entering the Temple[3], the Saviour was confronted, probably in the court of the Gentiles, with a scene of desecration, which called forth the first display of holy zeal for the dwelling-place of HIM, whom He had already declared to be His Father. For the convenience of Jews residing at a distance, who wished to offer sacrifice at the festivals, a kind of market had been established in the outer court, and here 'sacrificial victims, incense, oil, wine, and other things necessary for the service and the sacrifices, were to be obtained[4].' The common money, moreover, circulated in the country not being receivable within the Temple, the money-changers had set up their tables, in the same locality, to exchange all common and foreign coins for the sacred shekel, alone current in the sacred precincts. But

[1] Josephus, *B. J.* VI. 9. 3, estimates the number of lambs sacrificed at the Passover in the time of Nero at 256,500.

[2] For some striking remarks suggested by the presence of Jesus at the Jewish festivals, see Archer Butler's *Sermons*, 1st Series, p. 264.

[3] Jn. ii. 13—22. Of course it is assumed that this purgation of the temple is not to be identified with that mentioned in Matt. xxi. 12, &c.; Mark xi. 15, &c.; Luke xix. 45, &c. See S. Chrysost. *in Matt.* Hom. LXVII.; Ebrard's *Gospel History*, p. 379, E. T.

[4] See Tholuck's *Comm. on S. John*, p. 106, E. T.

together with such money-changing other business appears to have gradually crept in, and in place of the order and decorum that ought to have reigned undisturbed in such a spot, the noisy huckstering of merchants and traders disturbed the devotions of the worshippers, and converted the sanctuary of the Most High into a wrangling mart.

In the midst of a scene like this the Saviour entered the Temple. Few, perhaps, noticed Him as He entered amidst the train of pilgrims; none knew who was walking amongst them, or recognised in the lowly Stranger from Nazareth the 'Messenger of the Covenant[1].' But His eye no sooner rested on this scene of desecration, than, penetrated with holy zeal for the honour of God, He made a 'scourge of small cords[2],' and with this simple weapon, singly and alone, He drove forth the sheep and oxen, overthrew the tables of the money-changers, poured out their unholy gains, and with a voice of conscious authority bade even those 'who sold doves,' offerings such as His own mother had once presented, to 'take these things hence,' and not 'make His Father's House a house of merchandize.' The tone, the look, the bearing of the humble Teacher of Galilee are not described, for the Evangelists aim not at effect, but the desired result was instantaneous. Awed by that Presence[3], that calm Majesty, the dese-

[1] Malachi iii. 1.

[2] On this significant incident which Bauer deems so unsuitable, see Ebrard's *Gospel History*, p. 219.

[3] For other indications of the impression produced at times by the appearance and words of the Saviour, see John vii. 46, Οὐδέποτε

crators of the Temple left the scene of their unholy traffic.

But this was not all. Unable to resist the authority wherewith the mysterious Stranger spake, wondering, it may be, at those deep and marvellous words 'My Father's House,' now for the first time openly uttered in the ears of the people, the Jews approached Him in the midst of the now deserted Temple, and requested a 'sign,' the performance of some miracle or prodigy, in attestation of His right to 'do these things.' Nor was a 'sign' withheld; not, indeed, such a one as they looked for, but one which they never forgot, and which, though the disciples did not understand it at the time in all its deep meaning, was afterwards more plainly revealed. With that perfect calmness which ever distinguished Him, but without a syllable of explanation or comment on its meaning, the Holy One spake and said,

Destroy this Temple, and in three days I will raise it up[1].

Perplexed, astonished, the Jews replied, *Forty and six years was this Temple in building, and wilt Thou rear it up in three days?* But to this enquiry no answer appears to have been vouchsafed. They had asked for a 'sign,' and a sign had been vouchsafed, a 'parable,' a 'dark saying,' for their meditation and reflection. Even if we had not an inspired interpretation of these mysterious words, we might at least claim

ἐλάλησεν οὕτως ἄνθρωπος, according to reading of LT[Tr]. John xviii. 6, *Ὡς οὖν εἶπεν αὐτοῖς, Ἐγώ εἰμι, ἀπῆλθαν εἰς τὰ ὀπίσω, καὶ ἔπεσαν χαμαί.*

[1] Jn. ii. 19.

them as already shadowing forth a connexion between the speaker and that sacrificial ritual of which the Temple was the one only ordained centre.

But the interpretation of the Evangelist imparts a still greater importance to these words. '*He spake*, we read, *of the Temple of His Body*,' and then it is added, that when the Saviour arose from the dead, the Apostles recalled it to mind, and *believed the Scripture, and the word which Jesus had said*[1]. Now with this inspired interpretation to guide us, we can hardly exaggerate the importance of this 'sign' given to the Jews at the first Passover of the Saviour's official ministry. '*Destroy*,' said He, '*this Temple*.' The words are spoken prophetically and permissively. 'He prophesies in the beginning,' observes Stier, 'concerning the End, He unveils to the Jews, if perchance they might apprehend it by subsequent reflection, the entire relation of His sanctified Person to them and to their Temple Service; He tells them, as the Searcher of hearts, 'how well He knows that they themselves, who should be the defenders of the Temple, would be guilty of its destruction, and yet that by the marvellous prearrangement of the counsel of God, the evil which they should do to the Temple of His Body, would subserve at the same time to the removal of all shadows, and the resurrection of the new and abiding out of the death of the old[2].' But it does not concern

[1] Jn. ii. 22.

[2] Stier, I. 74 sq. IV. 361. He well observes that the later teaching of the New Testament as fully developed in the Epistle to the Hebrews '*is already wrapped up as a germ in this early word of our Lord*.'

us to press any particular interpretation of the words. The distinct connexion between the Saviour's Person and the Temple Ritual, here avowed openly at this first Passover is sufficient for our purpose. How widely this mysterious saying, though misunderstood, was circulated and how deep was the impression it made, is clear from several subsequent incidents. In a distorted form it reappeared in the mouths of the false witnesses in the hall of the high priest[1]; as a taunt and mockery it was flung in the teeth of the Holy One, as He hung upon the Cross; *They that passed by railed on Him, wagging their heads and saying, Ah, Thou that destroyest the Temple, and buildest it in three days, save Thyself, and come down from the Cross*[2].

But this was not the only incident that rendered this Passover memorable. The Saviour prolonged His stay at Jerusalem, and wrought more than one miracle[3], so that they who beheld them believed on His Name. Their faith, however, sprang from imperfect motives, and to them He would not entrust Himself, or unveil the mysteries of His Kingdom. Still even thus early there was one, a Pharisee and member of the Sanhedrim, named Nicodemus, whom a timid but real conscientiousness brought within the circle of his influence. This ruler, it is not improbable, had heard of the marvellous incident which had so lately occurred within the Temple-courts; he had also, it would seem[4],

[1] Matt. xxvi. 61; Mk. xiv. 58.

[2] Matt. xxvii. 39, 40; Mk. xv. 29.

[3] Θεωροῦντες αὐτοῦ τὰ σημεῖα ἃ ἐποίει. Jn. ii. 23.

[4] Jn. iii. 2.

been an eye-witness of one or more of those 'mighty works' which the Stranger from Nazareth had wrought, and he had come to the conclusion that He could be no ordinary person, that, unassisted by Divine Power, He could not perform such 'signs and wonders.'

So profound, indeed, was the impression made upon his mind, that in spite of his position, in spite of the risk he ran, in spite of the natural prejudices against so obscure a teacher, he resolved to seek Him out, and obtain an interview with Him, to go Himself, under cover of night indeed, but still to go, and ascertain who and what He was. And he found Him. '*Rabbi*,' he began, '*we know that Thou art a teacher come from God; for no man can do these miracles that Thou dost, unless God be with him*.' He had come resolved to recognise in the Galilean Stranger 'a Teacher sent from God,' and was prepared to hear, and perhaps accept His teaching. We all know what followed, we all know how the Holy One received this first enquirer, how in language utterly opposed to every popular predilection respecting the Messianic kingdom, He unfolded to His wondering hearer the mystery of a birth not *of the will of man, nor of the will of the flesh, but of Water and of the Holy Spirit*[1]. Into these momentous disclosures we are not concerned to enter now. We would only draw attention to the fact how again there fell from the lips of the Saviour words, which clearly prove that He had no dim or uncertain consciousness of the Way and Goal of His life. To the ruler's perplexed enquiry,

[1] Jn. iii. 5—8.

'how could the things be' of which he had heard? He replied,

If I have told you earthly things, and ye believe not, how shall ye believe, if I tell you of heavenly things? And no man hath ascended up to heaven, but He that came down from heaven, even the Son of Man which is in heaven. And as Moses[1] *lifted up the serpent in the wilderness, so must the Son of Man be lifted up: that whosoever believeth in Him should not perish, but have eternal life. For God so loved the world, that He gave His only begotten Son, that whosoever believeth in Him should not perish, but have everlasting life*[2].

A marvellous revelation this to a member of the Sanhedrim, a 'teacher of Israel,' well instructed, doubtless, in the Law and the Prophets! Did he, in common with his nation, cherish fond hopes of the Messiah's coming? Had these hopes in some measure prompted this secret interview? Was he looking forward to the fulfilment of the prophecies of Daniel, and expecting the days of the 'Son of Man'? He did well. But did not even Daniel speak of a '*Messiah to be cut off*[3],' and the cessation of the daily sacrifice? Was this inexplicable? Let the 'teacher of Israel' recall to mind his own 'Law.' Could he not remember a period when the ancestors of his nation were wanderers in

[1] 'Est hæc *prima* quæ a Domino facta legitur, *Mosis* mentio.' Bengel.

[2] Jn. iii. 12—16.

[3] Dan. ix. 26. On the attention paid by the Jews in his day to the prophecies, see Josephus, *Ant.* x. 11. 7.

the desert, when, denied a passage through the territory of the Edomites, they were fain to take a long and weary circuit over a sandy, shadeless desert, and, overcome with the trials of the way, brake out into bitter complaints against their leader, their hot toilsome march, and their food? Did he not remember how, as a punishment for their faithlessness, the deadly serpents[1] that infested the neighbourhood were sent amongst them, and destroyed many of them? And then, on the first signs of true repentance, did he not remember how the nation's leader was bidden to construct a Brazen Serpent, to set it on a pole, and uplift it before the eyes of the sufferers, and how, as many as looked thereon in the midst of their agonies were healed? Now, 'as Moses,' that Moses whose writings he studied and expounded, 'lifted up[2] that Serpent in the wilderness,' as a symbol of deliverance, or pledge of healing, 'so *must the Son of Man be lifted up*,' to the end that whoso believeth in Him may have—not the brief life that was restored to the tortured Israelites—but 'life eternal.'

How far the Jewish ruler entered into the full meaning of this strange unlooked-for intimation, how far it served to stimulate his mind to still deeper en-

[1] Numb. xxi. 7—9.

[2] 'There is even a significance in the word *lifted up;* the Lord used probably זקף, which in older Hebrew meant to lift up in the widest sense, but began in the Aramaic to have the restricted meaning of lifting up for punishment.' Tholuck, quoted in Article on *Saviour*, Smith's *Bib. Dict.* III. 1156; Ebrard's *Gospel History*, p. 222, note.

quiries into 'the Law and the Prophets[1],' whether on another memorable evening, when that 'lifting up' had actually been realized, it recurred to his mind as with another secret disciple he helped to consign the lacerated Body of the 'Son of Man' to the tomb[2], we cannot tell. What we *are* concerned to notice is the marvellous blending of wisdom and love in the intimation here given to the enquiring ruler. To have told him that the 'Son of Man,' with whom he could not fail to identify the 'Messiah,' was destined to be crucified and to die, would have been to tell him what he could then no more 'bear to hear' than the Apostles afterwards. But a 'sign' was given him[3], a deep prophetic intimation, sufficient to stimulate enquiry, and prepare him for the 'offence' of the Cross. Does this read like a mythical narrative? Do these words so calm, so deliberate, suggest the idea of an enthusiast? What have

[1] Comp. Wisdom xvi. 6, 7. 'The Targum of Jonathan paraphrases Numb. xxi. 8, "He shall be healed, if he direct his heart to the name of the Word of the Lord." If this paraphrase represents as it does the current interpretation of the schools of Jerusalem, the devout Rabbi, to whom the words were spoken, could not have been ignorant of it. The new Teacher carried the lesson a step further. He led him to identify the "Name of the Word of the Lord" with that of the Son of Man. He prepared him to see in the lifting up of the crucifixion that which should answer in its power to heal and save to the serpent in the wilderness.' Article *Brazen Serpent* in Smith's *Bibl. Dict.;* see also Kurtz's *Old Covenant,* III. 356; Stier, III. 441.

[2] Matt. xxvii. 57—61 and the parallels.

[3] Τὸ μὲν πάθος οὐ σφόδρα γυμνῶς τίθησιν, ἀλλὰ συνεσκιασμένως. S. Chrysost. *Hom. in Joann.* XXVII. Quid est serpens exaltatus? Mors Domini in Cruce. Mors Serpentis lethalis, mors Domini vitalis. S. Augustine *in Joann. Evang.* Tract. XII.

we here thus early in the public life of the Holy One? Thoughts of triumph, of kingdoms, of national glory? None of these—a *lifting up of the Son of Man,* not which *may* be, not which *peradventure* shall come to pass, but which *must* be, the *must* of a *foreknown* and *fully understood* necessity.

But from this eventful Passover, so fertile in deep and mysterious teaching, we must now pass on to another even still more momentous foreshadowing of the Passion. A year elapsed, and again the Paschal season drew nigh. During the interval[1] the fame of the Saviour had spread abroad far and wide. He was no longer the unknown teacher of Nazareth. His sphere of activity had been greatly enlarged. He had called His Apostles, delivered the sermon on the Mount, and laid down the laws of His kingdom. By many infallible signs He had proved that He 'came forth from God.' He had healed the nobleman's son at Capernaum[2], had restored the cripple at the pool of Bethesda[3], had raised Peter's wife's mother from her fever-stricken bed[4], had brought back to life the widow's Son of Nain[5], and the daughter of Jairus, had healed the centurion's servant[6], had stilled the tempest on the lake of Gennesareth[7], and released many that were possessed with demons. In

[1] With Anger, Wieseler, Tischendorf, and other eminent authorities we regard the feast mentioned in S. John v. 1 as the Feast of Purim.

[2] Jn. iv. 46—54. See Tischendorf's *Synopsis Evangelica.*

[3] Jn. v. 1—10.

[4] Mk. i. 29—31; Lk. iv. 38.

[5] Lk. vii. 11—17.

[6] Matt. viii. 5—13; Lk. vii. 1—10.

[7] Lk. viii. 22—25 and the parallels.

direct contrast to the mode of a mere Wonder-worker and the prevailing 'sign-seeking' of the age[1], His Redemptive 'works' had displayed an intimate connexion with the deep purpose of His mission[2]. Over disordered Nature, over the world of spirits, over disease, over death, He had proved Himself supreme, and attested the perfect subjection to Himself of all the evils that had gained a hold of the world since the first inroad of sin[3]. There is a harmony, a congruity about His miracles with His office as a Redeemer, to which the popular Messianic ideas could never have attained.

But during this year of ceaseless activity no further intimations had been vouchsafed respecting the goal and purport of His life. Now, however, as the fourth Evangelist expressly records, another Passover of His public ministry was 'drawing nigh[4].' On this occasion the Saviour does not appear to have gone up to Jeru-

[1] Lk. iv. 31—37; Lk. viii. 26—39, and parallels.

[2] See *Aids to Faith*, p. 21. And moreover they are exactly the kind of miracles which the popular imagination would *not* have attributed to the Messiah; there is about them a unity of purpose, an absence of all selfishness and self-display irreconcilable with such an idea.

[3] 'Among these miracles there are no portents—such as are related by classic writers; there are no exhibitions of things monstrous; there are no contrarieties to the order of nature; there is nothing prodigious, there is nothing grotesque. Nor among them are there any of that kind that might be called THEATRIC. There are no displays of supernatural power, made in the presence of thousands of the people summoned to witness them. Although claiming to be sent of God into the world, Christ did not, as Elijah had done, convene the people, and then challenge his enemies to dispute with him his mission by help of counter-attestations.' *Restoration of Belief*, p. 232.

[4] Jn. vi. 4.

salem. The determined hostility[1] of the ruling powers rendered any further activity in Judea dangerous, at least for the present, and He remained in Galilee. And here, having received intelligence of the death of His forerunner[2], and wishing to commune in quiet with His chosen twelve just returned from their first mission[3], He left Capernaum, and crossing the lake of Gennesareth, sought the neighbourhood of Bethsaida-Julias[4].

But the desired solitude was not to be obtained. Numbers moving about the country in consequence of the near approach of the Paschal Festival 'came on foot from all the towns round about[5] to see and hear Him.' The sight of these multitudes, scattered as sheep without a shepherd, called forth the Saviour's deepest compassion, and He 'taught them many things[6].' On this occasion, however, He would minister not only to their spiritual but also to their temporal wants, and, as the evening drew on, having, as we may believe[7], already put a question to one of the Apostles

[1] Jn. vii. 1. *Οὐκ ἀνῆλθε δὲ εἰς τὸ Πάσχα νῦν, ἀλλ' εἰς τὴν Γαλιλαίαν, κἀκεῖθεν εἰς Καπερναούμ, ἠρέμα λοιπὸν ὑπεκλύων τὸν νόμον, ἀφορμὴν λαμβάνων ἀπὸ τῆς Ἰουδαϊκῆς πονηρίας.* Cramer's *Catena in Joann.*

[2] Matt. xiv. 12. Tischendorf's *Synopsis.* See Lange, *Life of Christ,* III. 158, E. T.

[3] Mk. vi. 30, 31; Lk. ix. 10.

[4] Lk. ix. 10. See 'Bethsaida' in Smith's *Dictionary of the Bible,* and Thomson's *Land and the Book,* p. 372.

[5] Matt. xiv. 13; Mk. vi. 32; Lk. ix. 11.

[6] Mk. vi. 34.

[7] Jn. vi. 5. See Trench *on the Miracles;* Cramer's *Catena in S. Joann.;* Andrews' *Life of our Lord upon the Earth,* p. 265.

calculated at once to try his faith[1], and prepare him for the coming wonder, He bade them marshal the multitudes in companies amid[2] the green grass at the north-east corner of the lake, and with the five barley loaves and the two small fishes, which a lad possessed, proceeded to perform the ever memorable miracle of 'feeding the five thousand[3].'

The details of the miracle do not need from us any lengthened notice. The impression it made was profound. Not only were the spectators convinced that He, who thus fed them 'in the wilderness,' was indeed 'the prophet that should come into the world,' but they were ready to 'take him by force, and *make Him a King*[4].' To defeat their design, the Saviour bade the Apostles take ship and cross over to the other side of the lake[5], while He retired alone 'to pray[6].' In solitary communion with His heavenly Father He remained till near the fourth watch of the night, when walking on the water He drew near to His terrified Apostles,

[1] Jn. vi. 6.

[2] Jn. vi. 10, *ἦν δὲ χόρτος πολὺς ἐν τῷ τόπῳ. ἦν γὰρ ὁ καιρὸς τῆς πόας, ἔαρος λοιπὸν ὄντος· ἐγγὺς γὰρ ἦν, φησὶ, τὸ Πάσχα.* Cyril Alex. in Cramer's *Catena*.

[3] If this miracle was, as some suppose, (see Tischendorf's *Synopsis*, XXXIII.; Ellicott's *Lectures*, p. 207), wrought on a Passover-eve, the significance of its connection with what followed is very striking.

[4] Jn. vi. 14, 15.

[5] For a simple explanation of the difficulties here, see Thomson, *Land and Book*, 372, 3.

[6] Matt. xiv. 23; Mk. vi. 46. 'The second instance mentioned of a night so spent; the first being the night prior to the choice of the Apostles (Luke vi. 12, 13), and both mark important points in His life.' Andrews' *Life of our Lord upon the Earth*, p. 266.

who had been vainly striving to withstand the fury of the sudden storm[1] that swept the surface of the lake, and entering their little vessel accompanied them amidst the equally sudden calm to the other side, and the town of Capernaum.

There on the following day, a Sabbath it would seem[2], He repaired to the synagogue[3], whither He was before long followed by many of those who had beheld the miracle of the preceding evening. Marvelling how He had crossed the lake, they enquired when He had reached Capernaum, but received no direct answer to their question. As in the case of Nicodemus, the Holy One preferred to address Himself to their mental wants[4]. He knew the superficial character of their enthusiasm, He knew the temporal objects which had brought them in quest of Him. *Verily, verily, I say unto you,* He replied, *Ye seek me, not because ye saw*

[1] For a good description of one of these storms on the lake, see Thomson, *Land and Book*, pp. 374, 5.

[2] Though this is not absolutely certain. See Viner, *Real Worterbuch*, II. 549.

[3] The 15th of Nisan, according to Wieseler and other harmonists. Die sequenti (τῇ ἐπαύριον, vi. 22) et quidem sabbato loquitur enim in synagoga, (vi. 60) hanc disputationem a Jesu in synagoga Capharnaumi habitam esse dicit. Proficiscitur haud dubie ab eo die quo quinque millibus hominum cibum præbuerat. Est igitur dies sequens decimus quintus mensis Nisan, primus Paschatis dies festus. Accedit vero et lucis et gravitatis aliquid ab ejus diei festi dignitate ad hanc de edenda carne bibendoque sanguine Christi orationem. Tischendorf, *Synops. Evang.* XXXIV.; Ellicott's *Hulsean Lectures*, p. 210, and note. For a diverse opinion see Andrews' *Life of our Lord upon the Earth*, p. 270.

[4] 'Non respondet Jesus ad Judæorum *quando*, et sic sæpe in sermonibus ea, quæ series rerum et status animorum requirit, potius spectat, quam interpellationes loquentium alienas.' Bengel.

the miracles, but because ye did eat of the loaves, and were filled. Labour not for the meat which perisheth, but for the meat which endureth unto everlasting life, which the Son of Man shall give unto you: for Him hath God the Father sealed.

Apparently understanding the food 'that abideth for ever' in a literal sense, the people replied by asking *how* they might work the works of God, whereupon the Saviour declared that the work acceptable to God was[1] *to believe on Him whom He had sent.* To this they rejoined with that[2] insatiable craving for miracle after miracle, so characteristic of the merely carnal mind, *What sign showest Thou that we may see and believe Thee? what dost Thou work?* and then proceeded, as it seems, to suggest 'a work' and 'a sign from heaven,' such as they desired[3]. The miracle of the preceding evening had convinced many of them that the Speaker was indeed *the Prophet that should come into the world,* whose coming had been predicted by Moses. The great Lawgiver, then, they observed, *gave their fathers bread from heaven,* and that not once only, but during a space of forty years. Could *He* give them a 'sign from heaven' like that? In condescension to the associations they had themselves recalled, the Saviour replied that Moses had not given them the Bread from heaven, but His Father was giving[4] them the true

[1] Jn. vi. 29.

[2] Lücke quoted by Tholuck on S. John, p. 198, E. T.

[3] In exact correspondence with the popular hope of the highest temporal prosperity under the Messiah's rule.

[4] Or 'was about to give'? Οὐ Μωϋσῆς ἔδωκεν (LTTr) *ὑμῖν τὸν*

Bread from heaven, *for the Bread of God is He which cometh down from heaven and giveth life unto the world.* Still understanding Him to speak of some miraculous life-sustaining food, the Jews begged that He would 'evermore give them that Bread,' whereupon, passing from indirect to direct assertions, He replied in the ever-memorable words,

I am the Bread of Life[1],

and in words majestic in their very simplicity proceeded to vindicate His Divine nature, and His descent from heaven. This last assertion gave great offence to His hearers; they called to mind the earthly parentage of the Speaker, and marvelled how He could claim a Divine origin. But unmoved, undeterred by the increasing discontent, calm and unruffled, 'as if He felt Himself more truly addressing the ages to come, as if He stood in the presence, not of a few contentious disputants, but of the Church He was to found and to redeem,' the Holy One went on, whether they would hear or whether they would forbear:

I am the Bread of Life; your fathers did eat manna in the wilderness and are dead. This is the Bread which cometh down from heaven, that a man may eat thereof and not die. I am the Living Bread which came down from heaven: if any man eat of this Bread, he shall live for ever. And the Bread that I will give is My Flesh, which I will give for the life of the world[2].

ἄρτον ἐκ τοῦ οὐρανοῦ· ἀλλ' ὁ πατήρ μου δίδωσιν ὑμῖν τὸν ἄρτον ἐκ τοῦ οὐρανοῦ τὸν ἀληθινόν, Jn. vi. 32. For ἀληθινός as contrasted with ἀληθής, see Trench, *Synonyms*, Part I. 28—32.

[1] Jn. vi. 35. [2] Jn. vi. 47—51.

These mysterious words provoked still greater opposition on the part of the Jews; they *strove with one another*[1], saying, *how can this man give us His flesh to eat?* But their opposition moved not the calm majesty of the Holy One; with the same formula[2] of solemnity He had already thrice repeated, He resumed in words still more emphatic,

Verily, verily, I say unto you, Except ye eat the Flesh of the Son of Man, and drink His Blood, ye have no life in you. Whoso eateth My Flesh, and drinketh My Blood, hath eternal life, and I will raise him up at the last day. For My Flesh is meat indeed, and My Blood is drink indeed. He that eateth My Flesh and drinketh My Blood dwelleth in Me and I in Him. As the living Father hath sent Me, and I live by the Father: so he that eateth Me, even he shall live by Me. This is that Bread that came down from heaven; not as your fathers did eat manna, and are dead: he that eateth of this Bread shall live for ever[3].

Such were the momentous words the Holy One gave utterance to on this solemn occasion, at the season of the second Passover of His public ministry, words such as it is inconceivable any mere man could have spoken, which from the lips of a merely human teacher have no meaning whatsoever, which in their indefinable calmness transcend all possibility of confusion with human utterances. Without stirring the

[1] Ἐμάχοντο πρὸς ἀλλήλους. Jn. vi. 52.

[2] Ἀμὴν, ἀμὴν λέγω ὑμῖν, v. 33.

[3] Jn. vi. 53—58.

dust of the many controversies they have evoked, we may look at them in their broad and general bearings.

i. Regard the expressions here used from what point we will, we cannot but recognise their harmony with the intimations that distinguished the first Passover. Addressed to men who, the evening before, had witnessed the Speaker's creative power over natural bread, addressed in a sacrificial age to men who lived and moved in the midst of sacrificial scenes, the import of the words here used is of the most momentous character[1]. ii. Looking at them even from the stand-point of those who first heard them, and not throwing upon them the full light afforded by subsequent events, we cannot fail to recognise in them a progressive development of the revelations touching the innermost purport of the mission of the Holy One[2]. He who, at the first Passover, had intimated to Nicodemus that as *Moses lifted up the serpent in the wilderness, so must the Son of Man be lifted up, to the end that all that believe in Him may have everlasting life,* now distinctly announces Himself as '*the Bread of Life,*' as '*the Bread that came down from heaven,*' declares that 'the Bread which He will give is *His Flesh,* which He will give *for the life of the world,*' and with participation in '*His Flesh and Blood*' He connects the highest spiritual blessings[3].

[1] See Lange *on S. Luke,* I. p. 302, E. T.

[2] 'Tota hæc de carne et sanguine J. C. oratio *passionem* spectat, et *cum ea* S. Cœnam.' Bengel.

[3] 'Fateor nihil hic dici quod non in Cœna figuretur ac vere præstetur fidelibus: adeoque S. Cœnam Christus quasi hujus concionis sigillum esse voluit.' Calvin, quoted in Lange's *Life of Christ,* III. 152, n.

Taken together these intimations plainly point to something to come, something which though unintelligible to a Nicodemus, or the Jews of Capernaum, was quite intelligible to Him who uttered them. Neither the open murmuring of those present in the synagogue, nor the desertion of many of His disciples[1] which these mysterious expressions provoked, deter Him from reiterating them. He has a clear prevision of the goal and end of His life, it is no 'afterthought' with Him, it is distinctly contemplated from the beginning. Disciples may forsake Him, and 'walk no more with Him[2],' but He cannot conceal the truth. Simon Peter may speak in the name of the Apostles, and in reply to His question, 'Will ye also go away?' answer, *Lord, to whom shall we go? Thou hast the words of eternal life, and we believe and are sure that Thou art the Christ[3], the Son of the living God,* but the assurance of their faithfulness is damped by the thought that there was a traitor[4] in their midst, who, though now for the first time mentioned, is clearly not now for the first time discovered.

With this solemn discourse at Capernaum may be said to close the intimations of His end vouchsafed by our Lord during the earlier period of His ministry. The first announcement of the mysterious import of the

[1] Jn. vi. 66. [2] Ibid.

[3] Jn. vi. 69, or, according to the reading approved by LTTr, ὁ ἅγιος τοῦ Θεοῦ, 'the Holy One of God.' See Alford, and Scrivener's *Greek Test.*

[4] Ἀπεκρίθη ὁ Ἰησοῦς, Οὐκ ἐγὼ ὑμᾶς τοὺς δώδεκα ἐξελεξάμην, καὶ ἐξ ὑμῶν εἷς διάβολός ἐστιν. 'Did not *I* (myself), select you twelve, and one of you is a devil?' John vi. 76.

name of the child *Jesus* has already received a consistent and orderly development. 'In sundry times' and 'in divers manners,' without any trace of contrivance or logical adaptation, the one idea of a Saviour from sin has been preserved. There is no sign of any change of purpose as we go on. The popular Messianic ideas of glory and triumph are not gradually exchanged for sadder strains[1]. Already has the deepest purport of His mission been declared to be the delivery of 'His people from their sin;' already has the aged Simeon foreseen sorrow and heart-piercing anguish in store for His mother; already the Baptist has twice pointed Him out as the 'Lamb of God' who is to 'take away the sin of the world;' already at the first Passover of His public ministry has He given deep prophetic hints of something to befall Himself, of a 'Temple to be destroyed and rebuilt in three days,' of a 'lifting up like the serpent in the wilderness;' already every one of His marvellous works is clearly seen to be in complete harmony with the revealed purport of His mission; already, on the occasion of the second Passover, He has declared that He is the 'Bread from heaven,' that He is about to give His human flesh[2] 'for the life of

[1] 'The obscure predictions in John were in perfect correspondence with the situations in which they were uttered, in so far as Jesus uttered them before persons standing at a greater distance from Him, or in larger assemblages, or not in the form of categorical disclosures, but in connection with other disclosures.' Lange, III. p. 249, E. T.

[2] *Καὶ ἀποθνήσκω, φησίν, ὑπὲρ πάντων, ἵνα πάντας ζωοποιήσω δι' ἐμαυτοῦ, καὶ ἀντίλυτρον τῆς ἁπάντων σαρκὸς τὴν ἐμὴν ἐποιησάμην.* Cyril Alex. in Cramer's *Catena.* On *σὰρξ* here used, see Ellicott's *Lectures*, p. 212, n.

the world,' that His flesh is 'meat indeed,' and His blood 'drink indeed.'

These may be said to be obscure intimations, but they are couched in language too expressive to be forgotten, and they *are consistent from first to last.* As we pass on to the later period of the Saviour's life we shall observe the same orderly progress in the revelations made, and shall see how with infinite wisdom and love the Apostles, convinced that He whom they had given up everything to follow was the Christ 'the Holy One of God,' were prepared to connect with His death the chief source of the blessings He came to bestow on them and on the world at large[1].

[1] 'Evangelium in duas partes potest dividi, ex quibus divina Jesu methodus elucet. Prior propositi est, *Jesus est Christus;* altera *Christum oportet pati mori, et resurgere.* Homines sæpe omnia simul docent: non item Sapientia Divina.' Bengel.

CHAPTER VI.

THE LATER MINISTRY.

Οἱ ὀφθέντες ἐν δόξῃ ἔλεγον τὴν ἔξοδον αὐτοῦ ἣν ἔμελλε πληροῦν ἐν Ἱερουσαλήμ.

S. Luke ix. 31.

Up to this time the intimations of the Saviour respecting the mournful close of His life had been mainly figurative and metaphorical. They had also been made not so much immediately *to* the Apostles as *in their hearing.* But with the commencement of the last year of His public life, there is a perceptible change in the character of the intimations of the End. The Holy One speaks to 'His own,' to those 'He Himself had chosen out of the world,' not in 'figures' or 'parables,' but clearly and openly. Metaphorical allusions give place to precise statements, and general to special declarations.

The first of these would appear to have been vouchsafed a few weeks after the memorable discourse in the synagogue of Capernaum. During the intervening period, the Saviour had proceeded with His disciples into the extreme northern parts of Galilee, had visited the neighbourhood of Tyre and Sidon[1], and preached the word in the midst of the half-pagan Decapolis. Works of mercy had, as always, accompanied Him wherever He went. The demon had been expelled from the daughter 'of the woman of Canaan[2];' the tongue of a dumb man had been loosed, and 'his ears opened[3];' four thousand men 'besides women and children' had been fed with seven loaves and a few fishes[4]; and where-ever the Apostles had followed their Master, they had listened to the outpouring of grateful thanks to 'the God of Israel' from the mouths of many healed by the Holy One of various infirmities[5]. Pharisees and Sadducees had approached Him and requested a 'sign from heaven[6],' and had been bidden to meditate 'on the sign of Jonas' the prophet[7], a sign afterwards more fully developed, and singularly in harmony with the tenour of a direct intimation about to be made to the Chosen Twelve.

For now having travelled in all probability along the eastern banks of the Jordan and beyond the lake of Merom, the Apostles reached the confines of Cæsarea Philippi. Here, on one occasion, they found their Master engaged in solitary prayer[8], a solemn and sig-

[1] Matt. xv. 21; Mk. vii. 24.

[2] Matt. xv. 21—28; Mk. vii. 24—30.

[3] Mk. vii. 31—37.

[4] Matt. xv. 32—38; Mk. viii. 1—9.

[5] Matt. xv. 30, 31. [6] Matt. xvi. 1. [7] Matt. xvi. 4.

[8] Lk. ix. 18, *ἐν τῷ εἶναι αὐτὸν προσευχόμενον κατὰ μόνας.* 'Jesus Patrem rogarat, ut discipulis se revelaret. Nam argumentum precum Jesu colligi potest ex sermonibus actionibusque insecutis.' Bengel.

nificant action, the precursor of not a few important events[1], as, on this occasion, of an important revelation. For, as they resumed their journey[2], He addressed to them the formal enquiry, 'Whom do men say that I am?' This was not an ordinary question. The Holy One was speaking to men who had been now for some time His constant companions, hearers of His words and spectators of the signs which accompanied them. He seems to have wished to ascertain from their own lips the result of those labours which now, in one sense, were drawing to a close, and thence to pass on to the second and principal part of His discourses with them[3]. To this enquiry, then, the Apostles replied, in words reflecting the various opinions then held amongst the people; *Some say John the Baptist, others Elias, others Jeremias, or one of the prophets*[4]. 'But,' continued the Holy One, *whom say* ye *that I am?* To this the Apostle Peter, speaking in the name of the rest, made the ever-memorable reply, *Thou art the Christ, the Son of the living God.*

The object for which the question had been put was now partly achieved. By the mouth of one of their number the Apostles had given utterance to their

[1] i. The *Baptism* (Lk. iii. 21); ii. The *Election of the Twelve* (Lk. vi. 12, 13); iii. The *Discourse in the Synagogue of Capernaum* (Matt. xiv. 23); see above, p. 78 and note; iv. The *Transfiguration* (Lk. ix. 28); v. The *Agony* (Lk. xxii. 44).

[2] *καὶ ἐν τῇ ὁδῷ ἐπηρώτα*, Mk. viii. 27.

[3] See Stier, II. 329, E. T.; Lange's *Life of Christ*, III. 229, E. T.

[4] See Lightfoot *on S. John* i. 25 as to the belief of the Jews that the prophets would rise again at the coming of the Messiah.

own deepest convictions, had expressed the conclusion to which they had come after so long enjoying the society of their Master. This outspoken testimony to His Messiahship and Divine Nature, so far exceeding all the common Jewish conceptions, the Saviour accepted; He acknowledged the truth of the Apostle's confession; He declared that it had not been revealed to him by 'flesh and blood,' but by His Father in heaven; He bestowed upon him the promise of peculiar dignity in the Church He was about to establish. But it was now, after strictly charging them not to divulge the fact that He was the Messiah to the world at large[1], that He began clearly and distinctly to reveal to them the 'things concerning Himself.' *The Son of Man*, He declared, *must go up to Jerusalem, and there suffer many things from the elders, chief priests, and scribes, and be put to death, and after three days rise again*[2]. This was the first intimation, clear, distinct, and peremptory, of what lay before Him. He announces not only who will be the agents in His sufferings, but the form they will take, the place where He will undergo them, and their issue, a resurrection on the third day[3]. These events are not spoken of as a possibility, or a probability, a peradventure, or a chance, He says not the Son of Man 'may' go, or 'will' go to Jerusalem; He says that He '*must*' go. He speaks of it as a condition of His existence well understood, as the fulfilment of an eternal purpose.

[1] Mk. viii. 30. [2] Matt. xvi. 21; Mk. viii. 31; Lk. ix. 21, 22.
[3] See Lange on Lk. ix. 9.

How the announcement was received by the Apostles is familiar to every one. The self-same Peter, who a moment before had witnessed so noble and outspoken a confession to His Lord's Divinity, was utterly unable to endure even the thought of His sufferings. *That be far from thee, Lord,* was his indignant reply. But a solemn rebuke checked at once his untimely expostulations, which savoured of the weakness of flesh and blood, not of holy obedience to a heavenly Father's will. The same resolution which had triumphed over the more direct temptations of the wilderness triumphs over this no less subtle temptation. Nay, more, as if to seal the words He had uttered in the presence of many witnesses, the Saviour called to Him[1] some of the people that were standing near, and in their hearing as well as that of the Apostles, bade all who would come after Him '*take up their Cross,*' the symbol of a degrading death now for the first time mentioned, and 'follow Him;' for through the Gate of Suffering lay the road to Glory not only for Himself, but all His followers.

Momentous as was the announcement made, calculated as it was to cause deep questionings in the hearts of the Apostles, it was followed by a still more remarkable event. To cheer, we may believe, the wounded spirits of the Apostles, to enable them by an outward act to understand the reality of what He had already revealed in speech, the Holy One assured them that there were some standing there who should

[1] Mk. viii. 34, *προσκαλεσάμενος τὸν ὄχλον σὺν τοῖς μαθηταῖς αὐτοῦ.*

not 'taste of death,' till they had seen the Son of Man, in spite of the sad announcement He had just made, 'coming in His kingdom[1].' And six days afterwards, with three of the most privileged of their number, who had already in the chamber of Jairus witnessed their Master's power over death, He retired to one of the numerous mountain-ranges in the neighbourhood, not improbably one of the summits of Hermon[2]. S. Luke informs us that one object of this withdrawal was that He might engage in solitary prayer[3]. The weariness of the three Apostles seems to indicate that evening was the time of this withdrawal[4], the close it may be of a long day spent in 'going about doing good.' While, then, they slept, and He continued engaged in prayer[5], a marvellous change came over their Lord[6]. His raiment suddenly became shining, *exceeding white as snow;* the fashion also of His countenance was altered, and *shone like the sun.* The chosen three, roused, it may be, by the supernatural brightness around them, awoke, and shaking off their slumbers, not only beheld the marvellous change which had come over their Lord, but per-

[1] Matt. xvi. 28; comp. Mk. ix. 1; Lk. ix. 27.

[2] See however Thomson, 433.

[3] Lk. ix. 28, *ἀνέβη εἰς τὸ ὄρος προσεύξασθαι.*

[4] Lk. ix. 32.

[5] Lk. ix. 29, *καὶ ἐγένετο ἐν τῷ προσεύχεσθαι αὐτόν.*

[6] The slightest attention to the original Greek proves that the occurrence here described was no 'waking vision' or 'dream.' 'Peter and they that were with him *had been weighed down by sleep* (ἦσαν βεβαρημένοι ὕπνῳ), but *they thoroughly roused themselves* (διαγρηγορήσαντες δὲ), and saw His glory and the two men standing with Him.' Luke ix. 32. See Alford *in loc.* and Stier, II. 365.

ceived also that He was no longer alone! He was accompanied by two men, in whom they were enabled to recognise no others than the great pillars and representatives of the Old Testament Economy, Moses and Elias. Nor did they only see their transfigured Lord attended by these strange visitants from the world of spirits, but they were privileged to overhear the subject of their mutual converse! And on what high theme, or what momentous topic were Moses and Elias thus conversing with their Master? 'They *spake of*[1], or 'described,' we read, *the decease He was about to accomplish at Jerusalem.*

Upon the ardent, impulsive Peter, it was the scene itself, and not the topic of mysterious converse that made the most impression. To him it seemed as though 'the kingdom of heaven' was indeed 'revealed in power;' in the excitement of the moment he would have detained the heavenly visitants; he would have made three tabernacles, one for his Lord, one for Moses, and one for Elias, in order that from thence the laws of the Kingdom should be promulgated, and all men should recognise the true Messiah attended by the Pillars of the old Economy. But it was not to be. While he was yet speaking, there came a cloud, not dark and lowering like that on Sinai, but light and luminous as

[1] Ἔλεγον τὴν ἔξοδον αὐτοῦ, Lk. ix. 31. 'An unusual construction of λέγειν,' it has been remarked, 'though it occurs again in Rom. iv. 6, and in the earliest Ecclesiastical writers, in the sense of "recounting," "relating the details of," "describing."' Westcott's *Introd. to the Study of the Gospels*, 298, n.

the Shechinah which filled the Temple, overshadowing them with its glory, and out of it there came a Voice saying, *This is My Beloved Son, hear ye Him.* And then all was over. While the Apostles lay panic-stricken on their faces, their Master once more joined them, and bade them 'rise and be not afraid,' and, as they descended from the mount, He charged them to reveal to no man what they had seen, till (again the mysterious words recurred) '*He should have risen from the dead*[1].'

The Transfiguration, which we need hardly remark we regard as a real objective fact, marks an important epoch alike in the history of our Lord, as also in the education of the Apostles. Perplexed and disheartened six days before by the emphatic announcement of their Master's coming sufferings, they had now beheld with their bodily eyes infallible proofs of His celestial dignity. Had they by the mouth of Peter declared that He was indeed the Messiah, 'the Son of the living God'? they had now seen Him clothed awhile in the robe of His heavenly glory, they had heard a Voice from a higher world attesting and confirming that Sonship in which they had declared their belief. But was this all? They had a few days before shrank from that clear but mournful announcement of degradation and death which He had declared to be in store for Him. But of what had they heard the august representatives of the Law and the Prophets conversing with Him?

[1] Matt. xvii. 9; Mk. ix. 9.

Had they described the glories of a mighty kingdom soon to be established? Had they spoken of a speedy revelation of earthly might and majesty, of the exaltation of the 'Israel of God' to a supremacy above all peoples and languages? Nay, the single subject of their mysterious converse was '*the decease*[1]' to be accomplished at Jerusalem; the very rejection and suffering which had so lately moved their indignation! The great pillars of the old Economy did not shrink from the contemplation of such a scene; they clearly regarded it as a subject of the deepest interest, as the fullest manifestation of their Master's glory! A Voice from heaven had emphatically declared *This is my beloved Son, hear ye Him,* and yet He was to 'accomplish a decease' at Jerusalem! Little as the chosen three understood the full meaning of these words at the time, we cannot fail to observe how perfectly it was adapted to enable them to connect with their Master's death at Jerusalem, when it *did* occur, an accomplishment of all that the Law or the Prophets had prefigured. One of them, we know, never forgot the scene he had now witnessed[2]. Long after the present occurrence, when the time of his own 'decease' was not far distant, there came back to him the remembrance of the lonely mountain, and his transfigured Lord; he could declare how with his own eyes he

[1] For the word ἔξοδος comp. Wisdom vii. 6; 2 Pet. i. 5. 'Res magna; vocabulum valde grave, quo continetur passio, crux, mors, resurrectio, ascensio.' Bengel.

[2] 2 Pet. i. 14.

had beheld His majesty, how with his own ears he had heard the heavenly Voice[1]; he 'knew Him in whom he believed,' and He was not ashamed to seal his faith with his blood.

And now that the first open intimation of the Passion has been uttered, now that in the presence of the great representatives of the old Economy the Holy One has been consecrated to His sufferings, the difference between the earlier and later communications becomes more and more perceptible. Do the Chosen Three marvelling at the disappearance of Elias enquire how the scribes can affirm that the coming of Elias is to precede that of the Messiah? He replies by enquiring how it could be written 'of the Son of Man, that He must suffer many things and be set at nought[2]?' thus directing their attention to the many passages in the Old Testament foretelling a suffering Messiah. Do the Apostles[3] marvel at the power wherewith He heals the lunatic youth, whom their own efforts had failed to cure? He calms their excitement by repeating the former announcement of coming sufferings, and bids them let His words[4] 'sink down into their ears,' for 'the Son of Man was about to be betrayed into the hands of men, and be killed, and rise again on the third day.' Though the full force of His words were still as much hidden from them, though they feared[5] to ask for further information, the fact that He should

[1] 2 Pet. i. 17, 18. [2] Mk. ix. 12; Matt. xvii. 10.
[3] Lk. ix. 43, πάντων δὲ θαυμαζόντων ἐπὶ πᾶσιν οἷς ἐποίει.
[4] Lk. ix. 44. [5] Mk. ix. 31, 32.

suffer does not therefore the less form a part of His *distinct* teaching. Nor is it in their hearing only that He dwells on the same mysterious theme. The season of the Feast of Tabernacles comes round, and He goes up to Jerusalem. In the midst of His teaching in the temple the thought of His coming removal recurs, and in the presence of marvelling listeners He declares, *Yet a little while am I with you, and then I go unto Him that sent Me. Ye shall seek Me, and shall not find Me: and where I am, thither ye cannot come*[1]. These words naturally gave rise to much enquiry and discussion amongst the Jews, and when for the second time during the Feast He expressed Himself to the same effect, they scornfully enquired whether He intended to kill Himself, when He said, *Whither I go, ye cannot come*[2]. But their contempt ruffled not for a moment His unearthly composure. He calmly reiterated what He had already said with the important addition, *when ye shall have lifted up the Son of Man, then shall ye know that I am, and that I do nothing of Myself*[3]. The same expression which had been already used, an expression based upon common phraseology, in the hearing of Nicodemus, is now used publicly in a discourse in the Temple.

But a few days afterwards the Holy One made a still more striking announcement. Taking occasion from the familiar associations of the shepherd's life, He proclaimed Himself '*the good*,' the true, the real *Shepherd*[4].

[1] Jn. vii. 33, 34. [2] Jn. viii. 21, 22. [3] Jn. viii. 28.

[4] Jn. x. 11, ὁ ποιμὴν ὁ καλός. Compare the use of καλός in 1 Tim. iv. 6.; 1 Pet. iv. 10; 2 Tim. ii. 3.

I am the Good Shepherd, He declared, *and know My sheep, and am known of Mine. As the Father knoweth Me, even so know I the Father: and I lay down My life for the sheep: and other sheep I have, which are not of this fold: them also I must bring, and they shall hear My voice, and there shall be one fold, and one Shepherd.* Nay more, He affirmed that because He was about to lay down His life, *therefore*[1] the Father loved Him, but even in the mystery of His voluntary self-sacrifice He and the Father were one, that in laying down His life, He did it of His own free will, unconstrained by any human compulsion, for *He had power to lay it down, and power to take it again*[2].

We cannot marvel that the calm sublimity of the discourse in which these words occur made a deep impression on those who heard it, that 'the mixed multitude, the dwellers at Jerusalem[3], the officials of the Temple[4], and to some extent the hostile Jewish party[5], bore witness to the more than mortal power of the teaching of Jesus of Nazareth[6].' Verily either He who gave utterance to these words was what the Evangelists declare, and the Church in all ages has believed Him to have been, or they have succeeded not only in giving form and substance to an ideal such as has never been realized before or since, but in putting into the

[1] Jn. x. 17. διὰ τοῦτο ὁ Πατήρ με ἀγαπᾷ, ὅτι ἐγὼ τίθημι τὴν ψυχήν μου. See Stier, v. 482. '*Amor Patris non modo erga nos, sed etiam erga Christum, in Passione Christi spectandus est; non solum severitas ultrix.*' Bengel.

[2] Jn. x. 17, 18. [3] Jn. vii. 25. [4] Jn. vii. 46.

[5] Jn. viii. 30. [6] Ellicott's *Hulsean Lectures*, p. 256.

mouth of the Speaker language combining an unutterable dignity and majesty with a simplicity, to which the whole range of literature presents no parallel; language which has been read for eighteen hundred years by thousands of all nations and tongues, of all classes and conditions, with an instinctive acknowledgment that 'never man spake like this Man.'

But from the Feast of Tabernacles let us pass on to the period immediately preceding the last Passover, for our limits forbid us to follow the Holy One during His farewell visits to Galilee and Samaria, or the villages of Peræa. A solemn earnestness marks every step in this closing period; the Saviour neither sought nor hastened the end which he Had foretold. Hypocritical Pharisees might send Him a friendly warning, that 'Herod is seeking to kill Him[1],' but their words ruffle not His spirit; He knows that His hour is not yet come, that 'to-day and to-morrow' He should cast forth demons, and work miracles, and on the third day 'be perfected,' for 'no prophet could perish out of Jerusalem.' Parables of touching beauty and appropriateness to this closing period, 'the Lost Sheep,' 'the Lost Coin,' 'the Prodigal Son,' fall from His lips[2], while in the restoration of Lazarus to life after being four days in the tomb, the disciples behold the crowning proof of His superhuman power, the last and greatest of His redemptive 'works[3].'

[1] Lk. xiii. 31—35.
[2] Lk. xv. 1—32. Tischendorf's *Synopsis*, p. 111.
[3] Jn. xi. 4—46.

At length the hour draws nigh, and the final journey towards Jerusalem is begun. For the third time, as He advances before His chosen Twelve with a dauntless resolution at which they are awed and amazed[1], He recounts to them all things that are to befall Him, with a minuteness exceeding any former revelation. *Behold*, saith He, *we go up to Jerusalem, and the Son of Man shall be delivered unto the chief priests, and unto the scribes, and they shall condemn Him to death, and shall deliver Him to the Gentiles: and they shall mock Him, and shall scourge Him, and shall spit upon Him, and shall kill Him, and*, for the thought of suffering is never dissociated from that of ultimate triumph, *the third day He shall rise again*[2]. It is a striking proof how utterly opposed to Jewish ideas was this prediction, that it was this period of all others which two of the Apostles, even two who had witnessed the Transfiguration, selected to request that in the kingdom they believed their Master about to set up they might sit *the one on His right hand, and the other on His left*[3]. They seem utterly unable to *conceive* the realization of His thrice-repeated announcements. Their thoughts are in perfect harmony with the expectations of their nation. Even the assurance that these two should *drink of His cup, and be baptized with His baptism*, sounds like the concession of some mysterious dignity, and provokes a jealousy on the part of the rest which the Holy One checks by reminding them once more of the true

[1] Mk. x. 32. [2] Mk. x. 33, 34 and the parallels.
[3] Matt. xx. 20—28; Mk. x. 35—45.

nature of His kingdom, that therein He is truly first who is the servant of all, *even as the Son of Man came not to be ministered unto, but to minister, and to give His life a ransom for many*[1].

With this final proof of the utter inability even of those He had Himself called around Him, to lighten by their sympathy a particle of what lay before Him, the Saviour continued His way, entered Jericho, accepted the hospitality of the publican Zaccheus[2], corrected, by delivering the parable of 'the Pounds,' the idea that the kingdom of God *was about immediately to appear*[3], and at length, six days before the Passover, reached the safe seclusion of the mountain hamlet of Bethany[4], where He spent His last earthly sabbath.

Here, in the house, it would seem, of one Simon[5] who had been a leper, and had not improbably been restored to health by the Saviour Himself, Mary and Martha provided a festal repast to welcome Him, who had in so signal a manner restored happiness to their little circle. But even this season of seclusion did not pass away without a significant proof how the thought of what was to come was uppermost in His mind. As the feast proceeded Mary approached, and in proof of her deep and overflowing love for Him who had restored her brother to life, anointed His head and feet with precious spikenard. But this act of beautiful

[1] καὶ δοῦναι τὴν ψυχὴν αὐτοῦ λύτρον ἀντὶ πολλῶν, Matt. xx. 28; Mk. x. 45.

[2] Lk. xix. 1—10.

[3] Lk. xix. 11.

[4] Matt. xxvi. 6—13; Mk. xiv. 3—9; Jn. xii. 1—11.

[5] Matt. xxvi. 6; Mk. xiv. 3.

affection won not the approval of all in the room. To some of the Apostles, and especially to Judas, it seemed utterly unbecoming that unguents, which might have fetched so much and have been given to the poor, should be wasted in a useless piece of extravagance, and they *had indignation*[1], and *murmured against her.* He, however, to whom she had thus manifested her affectionate adoration, suffered scarcely a moment to elapse before He signified *His* opinion of her conduct[2]. Not only, He declares, had she done nothing wrong, but she had wrought a beautiful and noble deed. The poor, for whom some pretended so much anxiety, they *had always with them*, but Himself they *would not have always*, thus reminding them of that speedy removal He had so often already announced. And then He proceeded to declare that what this woman had done, had a special and peculiar significance. In reference to the mysterious Event so soon about to befall Him, wherein He should receive so little assistance or comfort from any human being, she, at least, 'had done what she could;' *She hath come before hand*, said He, *to anoint My Body to the burying; Verily, verily, I say unto you, Wheresoever this Gospel shall be preached throughout the whole world, there shall also what this woman hath done be told for a memorial of her*[3]. Thus by a prophetic word He elevated, interpreted, and glorified this proof of affectionate love.

[1] Matt. xxvi. 8.
[2] Mk. xiv. 6.
[3] Matt. xxvi. 13; Mk. xiv. 9.

At length this eventful evening closed, and the next day dawned, the first day of the Holy Week. Leaving the seclusion of the quiet mountain-hamlet, attended not only by the little company of His own disciples, but by a constantly increasing crowd of pilgrims to the Festival[1], whom His fame and the late stupendous miracle at the tomb of Lazarus had attracted, the Saviour entered Jerusalem in meek triumph, *sitting on an ass, and a colt the foal of an ass*[2]. The whole city was moved to its very centre; filled with the conviction that at length Zion's king was truly come, thousands heralded His approach; garments were plucked off and cast down before Him, palm-branches were strawed in His way, 'Hosannas' rent the air, as in calm majesty He rode onwards recognized by thousands as the long-expected Messiah.

But how deep must have been the disappointment of all who looked for some great unmistakeable 'sign,' who expected to see Him claim the sceptre and ascend the throne, rewarding the general homage with some certain proof of His true character! Their homage was indeed accepted, but did He for a single moment, even in this hour of triumph, fall in with the popular expectations? A turn of the road, as He descended the slopes of Olivet, revealed the Holy City rising, 'as it were out of a deep abyss[3],' and presenting itself in all its glory before His eyes and those of His followers, and

[1] Jn. xii. 12.
[2] Mk. xi. 1—11 and the parallels; Jn. xii. 12—19.
[3] Stanley's *Sinai and Palestine*, 193.

the hour of *triumph* became the hour of deepest *sorrow*. The Holy One wept over the beautiful city; foresaw the hour of its desolation, the Roman legions gathered round its fated walls, its proud towers laid low in the dust, and its children within it, because it 'knew not the hour of its visitation!' The procession moved on to the city itself, and entered the Temple. Now at length, perhaps, some 'sign' will be vouchsafed. For the second time[1] the Holy Place of the Most High is cleansed of the mercenary crowd of traffickers, who have renewed their unholy occupation, making it *a den of thieves;* evening came on, and the Saviour retired once more to the little mountain hamlet, to the home of Martha and Mary and Lazarus! Marvellous rebuke, at every step, to the excited expectations of the people! On the assumption that He, who entered Jerusalem in this mysterious triumph, was the product of 'a heated popular imagination,' or a subtle combination of myths, what explanation is to be given of the minuteness which has recorded this significant rebuke of every popular prejudice, of every popular belief? Whence, if He was nothing more than this, the anxiety to embalm in words of unexampled pathos this signal discomfiture of a nation's hopes?

For a far different end from that which popular imagination could divine had the true Lamb of God

[1] Matt. xxi. 12—17; Mk. xi. 15—19; Lk. xix. 45—48. Many, as Greswell, Alford, Wieseler, see in this visit to the temple on the 10th of Nisan a fulfilment of the command (Exod. xii. 3—6) to select on this day a lamb for the Paschal sacrifice.

come up to this Paschal Festival. The ruling powers might harass Him from day to day with malicious questionings; Pharisees and Herodians respecting the duty of paying tribute to Cæsar[1]; the Sadducees with a frivolous objection to the doctrine of the Resurrection[2]; the Legalist with a difficulty respecting the relative greatness of the commandments[3], but while each disputant retired foiled and baffled, nor dared to ask Him any more questions; His own soul was filled with the thought of the real triumph now so near at hand[4]. We have a striking proof of this in a significant incident, which took place before the first half of the Holy Week[5] had passed away.

As He was teaching in one of the courts of the Temple, two of His Apostles, Andrew and Philip, approached Him with what they deemed a strange announcement. Amongst the thousands that crowded the Holy City were 'certain Greeks[6],' not Grecian Jews, nor even, it would seem, proselytes of righteousness, but heathens, and probably Greeks proper. In common with many others they had heard of the famed Teacher of Nazareth, of the mighty works He performed, of

[1] Matt. xxii. 15—22; Mk. xii. 13—17; Lk. xx. 20—26.

[2] Matt. xxii. 23—33; Mk. xii. 18—27; Lk. xx. 27—39.

[3] Matt. xxii. 34—40; Mk. xii. 28—34; Lk. xx. 40.

[4] Compare the parable of the *Wicked Husbandmen*, and Matt. xxi. 37; Mk. xii. 6—8; Lk. xx. 13—15.

[5] Some place this incident on the evening of the triumphal entry; others, as Robinson, Tischendorf, Wieseler, Ellicott, and Andrews, p. 363, on the Tuesday of the Holy Week.

[6] Jn. xii. 20. See Stier and Lightfoot, *in loc.*

the marvellous words that fell from His lips, and they wished to do something more than hear, they wished with their own eyes 'to see' this wondrous Teacher. But shrinking from approaching Him directly, they had applied to the apostle Philip[1], saying, *Sir, we would see Jesus.* Philip, seemingly perplexed, consulted Andrew, and together the two went and told their Lord[2].

And what said He, when He heard their announcement, when perchance He beheld these enquirers from the West? He instantly broke forth into words of mysterious joy[3]! '*The Hour,*' he declared, 'as if in a transport of holy rapture,' '*the Hour is come, that the Son of Man should be glorified. Verily, verily, I say unto you, Except a corn of wheat fall into the ground and die, it abideth alone: but if it die, it bringeth forth much fruit. He that loveth his life shall lose it; and he that hateth his life shall keep it unto life eternal. If any man serve Me, let him follow Me; and where I am, there will also My servant be; if any man serve Me, him will My Father honour*[4].

But with the thought of the seed-corn cast into the

[1] For the various reasons that have been assigned for their application to this Apostle, see Stier, VI. 77; Ellicott's *Lectures*, 316, n.

[2] Probably in the Court of the Women, into which no Gentiles would dare to intrude.

[3] 'Præludium regni Dei a Judæis ad gentes transituri.' Bengel. 'These men from the West represent at the end of Christ's life that which the wise men from the East represented at its beginning; but those come to the cross of the King, even as these came to His manger, and receive presently more full intelligence.' Stier, VI. 78.

[4] Jn. xii. 24—26. On the applicability of this figure to the Hellenic mind, see Stier, VI. 81; Lange's *Life of Christ*, 54—56, E. T.

ground and dying, came the thought of all that He must undergo. There fell upon Him the shadow of the dreadful Hour, and a sensible foretaste of Gethsemane[1] drew forth two of those deep mysterious exclamations which, unless our perceptions are only given to mock us, carry with them the conviction of the superhuman character of Him who uttered them. *Now is My soul troubled*, said He, *and what shall I say? Father, save Me from this hour.* And then, as though a cloud had rolled away, the perfectly willing Spirit spoke again, *For this cause came I unto this hour*[2]. *Father, glorify Thy name*[3]. But these words expressive of such deep, such infinite resignation were not to pass unheeded, they called forth the last of the Three Heavenly Voices, which, during His life on earth, attested the Divinity of the Saviour's mission. The voice which had been heard on the banks of Jordan, and on the mount of Transfiguration, is now heard in the courts of the Temple itself[4], saying responsively to the Saviour's significant utterance, *Father, glorify Thy name,...I have both glorified it, and will glorify it again.* Various were the interpretations of this mysterious utterance

[1] 'Concurrebat horror mortis, et ardor obedientiæ.' Bengel.

[2] '*Veni* in *hanc horam, ut venirem in hanc horam*, eamque *exantlarem*.' Bengel. See also Stier, VI. 85.

[3] Jn. xii. 27, 28.

[4] 'The third time had Jesus now solemnly announced His destiny of death; as first in the presence of the Baptist, the second time before the lawgiver and prophet of the Old Testament, so now in the holy place of sacrifice itself, in the tabernacle of God. And the third time does the Voice like thunder resound, by which the Father accredits the Son, and justifies His work.' Ebrard, quoted by Stier, VI. 89.

by the surrounding crowd. Some thought that it *thundered*, others, that *an angel spake to Him*[1]. But the Holy One Himself set all doubts at rest, saying, *This Voice came not because of Me, but for your sakes.* And then returned the same thoughts of triumph which the first announcement of the two Apostles and the sight of the enquiring Greeks, had called forth, *Now is the judgment of this world: now shall the Prince of this world be cast out, and I, if I be lifted up*[2], *will draw all men unto Me, signifying,* adds the Evangelist, *by what death He should die.*

With this last significant intimation, recalling by its associations the words addressed to Nicodemus two Passovers before, closes the cycle of announcements of the Passion previous to the institution of the Eucharist. On looking back we can discover no trace of any change of purpose, any alteration of plan, any 'sudden afterthought.' We have seen how the truth included in the first angelic message was gradually developed, how one idea pervades every intimation, every hint, every prophecy; how 'little by little' the minds of the Apostles were trained to receive the idea of a *suffering Messiah.* We have seen how the figurative and metaphorical allusions of the earlier period of the ministry made way for precise statements, and general for special declarations. Had the Holy One on the occasion of the first Paschal Festival of His public ministry spoken of the

[1] Comp. Acts ix. 4, 7, with xxii. 9 and xxvi. 14.

[2] Jn. xii. 32. Thus for the third time we have the figure of *lifting up.*

destruction and resurrection of the temple of His Body, and intimated to Nicodemus that as *Moses lifted up the serpent in the wilderness, so also the Son of Man must be lifted up?* Had He, when the same Festival again came round, spoke of Himself in the synagogue of Capernaum as the *True Bread from heaven,* declared that He was come *to give His life for the world,* and hinted at a mysterious *eating of His flesh,* and *drinking of His blood?* During the last year of His life we have seen these same announcements expanded and particularized. In the neighbourhood of Cæsarea Philippi we heard Him, after an Apostle had nobly declared his conviction of His Divine Nature, intimate for the first time clearly and unmistakeably the future that lay before Him, and the necessity for His going up to Jerusalem, and there being rejected and put to death; six days afterwards we heard the representatives of the Law and the Prophets conversing with Him touching '*the decease he was about to accomplish at Jerusalem;*' from this time we have seen the shadows deepen, and watched the earnestness with which He sought to prepare the Apostles for the End; we have heard Him publicly declare while teaching in the Temple, that the Son of Man *must be lifted up,* that for a little while He should remain, and then return to the Father; in various symbols borrowed from the world of men and the world of nature—the true and genuine Shepherd *who lays down His life for the sheep*—the ransom-money paid for the captive—the 'corn of wheat,' which must first be cast into the ground and *die before it can bring forth fruit;* we have heard Him speak of His death and its relation to the benefits He came to bestow upon the world; from the beginning to the end we have observed how the Apostles were trained *gradually and progressively* to realize the idea of His death, and prepared for the offence of the Cross.

CHAPTER VII.

THE INSTITUTION OF THE EUCHARIST.

Ἐπιθυμίᾳ ἐπεθύμησα τοῦτο τὸ Πασχὰ φαγεῖν μεθ' ὑμῶν πρὸ τοῦ με παθεῖν.

S. LUKE xxii. 15.

WE have now followed the Saviour wellnigh to the close of His life on earth. Again the Feast of the Passover drew near. Again, as in so many former years, the pastures and hills around Jerusalem were whitened with flocks; again the thoroughfares, especially in the neighbourhood of the sheep-market, were crowded with a moving mass of helpless victims; again the city itself was thronged with strangers and pilgrims from every quarter of the then known world, who, whether Jews or proselytes, had come up with one accord to celebrate the great national festival, and commemorate the birthday of the chosen people and their deliverance from Egyptian bondage.

Of the various festivals of the Jewish Church, if we except those of later institution which commemorated the deliverance of the people from Haman and Antiochus Epiphanes[1], the Passover was the only one which rested on a distinctly historical basis. Year after year, from generation to generation, it had been celebrated, and with every celebration recalled, as in 'a living drama,' the great story of the national deliverance; a deliverance effected not *by* them but *for* them, not by their own might, but by the uplifted hand of Jehovah, in which they had not been *actors* but *passive spectators*, had *stood still and seen the salvation of God*[2]. Year after year, from generation to generation, it had recalled by its expressive rites the awful night, *when there was not a house* in Egypt, *from the firstborn of Pharaoh that sat on his throne unto the firstborn of the captive in the dungeon*[3], *where there was not one dead;* when the destroying angel *passed over* the houses of those Israelites, and those only, on the lintels and doorposts of which the blood of the Paschal lamb had been sprinkled, and where the flesh of the lamb itself had been eaten with bitter herbs and unleavened bread.

Under, therefore, its first and most obvious aspect the Passover commemorated a redemption from cruel and oppressive bondage, a redemption wrought solely by the outstretched arm of Jehovah, conditional, as regarded the Israelites, on the sacrifice of a lamb, the sprinkling of its blood on the doorposts of each house, and the slaying and eating of it by each Paschal company. In

[1] See Stanley's *Lectures on the Jewish Church*, p. 121.

[2] Ex. xiv. 13.

[3] Ex. xii. 29.

this festival the principle of *mediation* found its highest expression. The victim slain was in the strictest sense a sacrifice, and combined some of the chief features of the sin-offering and the peace-offering. It was presented before the brazen altar in the holy place[1], the fat was burned by the priest, and the blood sprinkled on the altar[2]. It was then not burned, or eaten by the priests only, but by all the people, who at this sacrificial feast[3]—the distinguishing feature of the peace or thank-offering—partook of the 'Table of the Lord,' and received the seal and pledge of their covenant-relation.

At this point it will, perhaps, be well to try and realize the manner in which this Paschal Feast was then celebrated by the Jews[4]. It will be, indeed, impossible to harmonize every detail with what was afterwards instituted by the Saviour, but we may be, in some measure, helped to understand the associations, amidst which the Eucharist originated.

The company at the Table, which might not be less than ten persons, usually included from ten to twenty, according to the family, or the number of strangers that might be present. They met in the evening and

[1] Deut. xvi. 5, 6.

[2] 2 Chron. xxx. 16; xxxv. 11.

[3] See Cudworth's *True notion of the Lord's Supper*, Wks. II. 831.

[4] The authorities consulted for the following notice of the Paschal ceremonies have been Buxtorf, *de Cœna Domini;* Lightfoot's *Temple Service; The Book of Jewish Ceremonies*, by Gamaliel Ben Pedahzur, pp. 51—56; Godwyn's *Moses and Aaron;* Freeman's *Principles of Divine Service*, Vol. II. pp. 29—39; Lange's *Commentary on St Matthew*, Vol. II. 435, 6.

reclined on couches, this being the usual posture then, as standing had been originally[1].

The rites of the feast were regulated according to the succession of four[2], sometimes five, cups of wine mixed with water, which were placed before the head of the house, or the most eminent guest, who was called the Celebrant, the President, or *Proclaimer of the Feast.*

i. When they had reclined, he began by taking one of the four cups of wine in his right hand, and pronounced the benediction over the wine and the feast, saying, *Blessed be Thou, O Lord our God, the King of the universe, who hast created the fruit of the vine*[3]. He then drank the first cup, and the remainder of the household followed his example.

ii. Water was then brought in, and he blessed for the washing of hands, and washed, followed by the rest.

iii. The table was next set out with the unleavened bread, the sauce called Charoseth, and the Paschal lamb, and the flesh of the *chagighah,* or feast-offerings.

iv. The proclaimer of the feast then blessed God for the fruits of the earth, and taking a portion of the

[1] See *Mishna Pesach,* 10 § 1.

[2] Buxtorf, *de Cœna Domini,* pp. 299, 300, Omnes in cœna Paschali oportet quatuor pocula bibere.

[3] For similar words used in the Synagogue Service for *Friday night,* when a cup of wine is brought to the reader, a blessing pronounced, with a remembrance made of the Exodus, and then the wine is distributed amongst the little children, see Pedazhur, p. 137. Also at the end of the *Sabbath Evening Service,* when a cup of wine is again brought in, see *Ibid.* pp. 184, 185. Jost, *Gesch. Judenth.* I. 180, quoted in Article *Synagogue* in Smith's *Bib. Dict.*

bitter herbs dipped it in the sop, and ate it with all who reclined at the table.

v. The *Haggadah* or *showing forth* now commenced, and the Celebrant declared the circumstances of the delivery from Egypt, as commanded in the Law[1]. Then the second cup of wine was filled, and a child, or proselyte, enquired[2], What mean ye by this service? To which reply was made, according to a prescribed formula, or liturgy: *The Passover which we eat is in respect that the Lord passed over the houses of our fathers in Egypt.* Holding up the bitter herbs, he went on, *These bitter herbs that we eat are in respect that the Egyptians made the lives of our fathers bitter in Egypt.* Then holding up the bread in his hand, he said, *This unleavened bread which we eat is in respect that the dough of our fathers had not time to be leavened, when the Lord appeared unto them, and redeemed them out of the hand of the enemy, therefore,* he continued, *are we bound to confess, to praise, to extol, to magnify, and to ascribe victory to Him, who did unto our fathers and to us all these signs, and who brought us forth from servitude to freedom, from sorrow to joy, from darkness to marvellous light, and therefore we say before Him, Hallelujah!* whereupon Psalms cxiii. and cxiv. were repeated, followed by a solemn blessing and drinking of the second cup.

vi. Then, after a second washing of hands, taking two of the unleavened cakes, the Celebrant broke one of them, pronouncing the consecration in these words:

[1] Ex. xii. 17; xiii. 8.

[2] Ex. xii. 26.

Blessed be Thou, O Lord our God, King of the universe, who bringest forth fruit out of the earth[1]. He next distributed a piece to each person around him, saying, *This is the bread of affliction which our fathers did eat in the land of Egypt.* All present then dipped the portions with the bitter herbs into the Charoseth and ate them.

vii. After a thanksgiving to God who commanded the eating of the Passover, they then ate the flesh of the lamb with the bread, and the master, lifting up his hands, blessed the third cup of wine, especially known as the *Cup of Blessing*, and handed it round to each person.

viii. Thanksgiving was now renewed for the food of which they had partaken, for the delivery from Egypt, the covenant of circumcision, and the law, and a fourth cup was filled and drunk, while the remainder of the Hallel, Psalms cxv—cxviii, was sung, whence the cup was known as the cup of Song.

ix. Occasionally a fifth cup was drunk, while Psalms cxx—cxxviii. were chanted, but no more.

Such, or nearly such, was the mode of celebrating the Passover in the time of the Saviour. Up till now it will be noticed that we have no *record* of any actual participation in a Paschal Meal by our Lord in company with

[1] Pedazhur p. 52. Alexander's Jewish Service, p. 9. For the Grace on ordinary occasions before eating bread, see Pedazhur, p. 282. 'Their Rabbies compare their tables, whilst they are at their meals, to the altars, whereon the offerings were laid in their Temples, and therefore they are commanded by the Rabbies to read a portion of some of the laws of sacrifices at every meal.' *Ibid.* pp. 92, 3.

His disciples. At the first Passover we are, indeed, told that He went up to Jerusalem, and we may infer that He conformed in all things to Jewish usages, but the Evangelists have not described the circumstances of any actual Paschal celebration.

But two days before the period at which we have now arrived, He Himself reminded His disciples of the approach of the Festival, saying, *Ye know that after two days is the Passover, and the Son of Man is betrayed to be crucified*[1]. He thus distinctly intimated the occasion, when the event so often already foretold would take place. The 'Hour' so often declared *to be at hand* was now specifically fixed and definitely connected with the chief *historical* Festival of the Jews. And not only did He thus direct the attention of the Apostles to the approach of the Passover, but in reply to the enquiry where He intended to celebrate it, He bade two of their number, Peter and John, go into the city, where they would meet a man bearing a pitcher of water, whom they were to follow to whatever house he should enter. To the owner[2] of this house they were to address the significant words, the Master saith, *My time is at hand; where is the guest-chamber where I may eat the Passover with My disciples?* on which the Apostles were told that the householder would show[3] them a

[1] Mtt. xxvi. 1, 2.

[2] Probably a believing follower. *Discipulus, sed non ex duodecim.* Bengel. See also Stier, VII. 77; Lange on Mtt. xxvi. 17. Ellicott's *Lectures*, 321, n.

[3] Mtt. xxvi. 18; Mk. xiv. 14; Lk. xxii. 11.

large upper-room furnished and prepared; there they were to make ready.

In contrast with the silence, which has been hitherto maintained respecting any actual celebration of the Paschal Feast by the Saviour, we cannot fail to notice the minute care with which He Himself directed its celebration now. Not only does He send two of His Apostles to make ready; not only does He describe the guide to the house, and the words they were to address to the householder, but He particularizes even the size and aspect of the upper-room he would show them. Such minute directions could not fail to make a deep impression upon the Apostles, and to deepen in their minds the conviction that in the approaching feast their Master had a profound and mysterious interest, that He distinctly contemplated, and looked forward to it. The fact that the room is described as already *furnished and prepared*[1] suggests that the searching for and putting away of leaven, so important a preliminary to the Passover, had already been carried out, and hence we may infer that the preparation made by the Apostles included the provision of the unleavened cakes, of the bitter herbs, and of the cups of wine; of everything in short that could be prepared on the day before the sacrifice of the Jewish Paschal lambs[2].

[1] ἀνώγαιον μέγα ἐστρωμένον ἕτοιμον, Mk. xiv. 15; Lk. xxii. 12.

[2] Into the vexed and extremely difficult question whether the meal of which the Saviour now partook was the Passover or an anticipation of it, it has not been thought necessary to enter here. For a conspectus of all the arguments on both sides, see Ebrard's *Gospel History*, 395—405; Lange, *Life of Christ*, Vol. IV. 158—271; Article *Passover* in

This done, they probably returned to their Lord, who later in the evening, when the hour was come[1], the compact between the traitor and the chief priests having already been made[2], left the little village of Bethany, and entered the upper-room with the twelve. They sat down or reclined, and the Saviour taking the place of Celebrant, or Head of the family, said, *with desire have I desired to eat this Passover with you before I suffer*[3]*: for I say unto you, I will no more eat thereof until it be fulfilled in the kingdom of God.* With these words He took a cup, the first cup we may believe, devoted usually to the announcement of the feast, and gave thanks, and said, *Take ye this and divide it amongst you; for I say unto you, I will not drink of the fruit of the vine*[4], *till the kingdom of God shall come.*

But even now, even in this solemn hour, the old contention touching priority again broke out among the Apostles. He, however, who during the whole of their mutual converse had ever borne so gently with

Smith's *Bib. Dict.;* Andrews' *Life of our Lord upon the Earth*, 368—397; Bp. Ellicott's *Hulsean Lectures*, 322 n.

[1] Lk. xxii. 14.

[2] Mtt. xxvi. 14—16; Mk. xiv. 10; Lk. xxii. 3—6.

[3] The stress upon the words *this Passover* and *before I suffer* is clear. 'It is as if He had said, Because I cannot eat of the proper Passover, therefore have I desired beforehand, in this form, to eat it with you, and this My desire is now fulfilled.' Freeman's *Principles of Divine Service*, II. 303. Stier, VII. 33. Ellicott, 323 n.

[4] This expression *fruit of the vine* occurs in the Evening Synagogue service, Pedazhur, 136, in the Sabbath Evening service, *ibid.* 184, in the ordinary Grace before drinking wine, *ibid.* 282, as well as the Paschal Festival, *ibid.* 51, 136.

their shortcomings, to repress so unseemly a dispute, and at the same time teach them in the most striking manner a lesson of humility, took upon Him the form of a servant, and girding Himself with a towel washed His disciples' feet[1].

This done the feast was resumed[2], and probably the second cup of wine was drunk. But soon the consciousness of the traitor's presence, already darkly intimated, so wrought upon the Saviour, that His inmost soul was deeply moved and troubled[3], and He testified and said, *Verily, verily, I say unto you, that one of you will betray me*[4]. This announcement excited great surprise and sorrow among the Apostles, and many were the earnest questionings, *Lord, is it I?* At length He gave a special and private indication to the disciple that reclined upon His bosom[5]. The sop was dipped and given to Judas Iscariot, who immediately left the room and went forth to execute his awful purpose. With his departure the Saviour was no more troubled in spirit, but brake forth into the same triumphant language[6], which we have already considered, when in the courts of the Temple

[1] Jn. xiii. 1—20. Whether this was usual before the Passover see Buxtorf, *de Cœna Domini*, p. 303, ed. 1662.

[2] Even if δείπνου γενομένου, Jn. xiii. 2, be the right reading, the meaning must be *when supper had begun*. Tischendorf and Tregelles read γινομένου.

[3] Jn. xiii. 21, ἐταράχθη τῷ πνεύματι.

[4] Jn. xiii. 21.

[5] Jn. xiii. 24—36.

[6] Truly in the harmony of our Lord's words now with those uttered in the presence of the Greeks, we have 'a life and a truth with which the subtlest combinations of thought could never have animated a mythical narrative.'

He heard of the request of the Greeks. *Now,* said He, *is the Son of Man glorified, and God is glorified in Him; if God is glorified in Him, God will also glorify Him in Himself, and will straightway glorify Him*[1].

Again the feast proceeded, and soon taking one of the unleavened cakes that had been placed before Him and giving thanks, probably in the usual words, He brake it, and gave it to His Apostles, saying,

Take, eat, This is My Body, which is given for you; do this in remembrance of Me[2].

Afterwards He took a cup of wine, in all probability the third cup and known as the Cup of Blessing, gave thanks, and gave it unto them, saying,

Drink ye all of this; for this cup is My Blood of the New Covenant, which is shed for you, for many, for the remission of sins; this do ye as oft as ye shall drink it in remembrance of Me[3].

After this, He conversed with His Apostles on the events that were soon to happen to Himself and them, of their desertion of Him at the most critical moment, the failure of their faith, and their dispersion each unto his own. And then, whereas at the usual Paschal Feast

[1] Jn. xiii. 31, 32.

[2] Τοῦτό ἐστι τὸ σῶμά μου (Mtt., Mk., Lk., 1 Cor. xi. 24), τὸ ὑπὲρ ὑμῶν διδόμενον (Lk.), τὸ ὑπὲρ ὑμῶν [κλώμενον] 1 Cor. xi. 24, τοῦτο ποιεῖτε εἰς τὴν ἐμὴν ἀνάμνησιν (1 Cor. xi. 24).

[3] Πίετε ἐξ αὐτοῦ πάντες (Mtt.), τοῦτο γάρ ἐστι τὸ αἷμά μου τῆς διαθήκης (Mtt., Mk.), ἡ καινὴ διαθήκη ἐν τῷ αἵματί μου (Lk.; 1 Cor. xi. 25), τὸ περὶ πολλῶν ἐκχυνόμενον (Mtt.), τὸ ἐκχυνόμενον ὑπὲρ πολλῶν (Mk.), τὸ ὑπὲρ ὑμῶν ἐκχυνόμενον (Lk.), εἰς ἄφεσιν ἁμαρτιῶν (Mtt.), τοῦτο ποιεῖτε, ὁσάκις ἂν πίνητε, εἰς τὴν ἐμὴν ἀνάμνησιν (1 Cor. xi. 25).

it had been customary to continue long in religious conversation on the great events of the Exodus and the national deliverance from Egypt, so now did the Saviour converse with the eleven of His own departure to the Father and the coming of the Comforter[1]; of Himself as the true Vine, and His disciples as the branches[2]; of the hatred of the world and its sin against Himself[3], of the trials which the Apostles must expect, and the assured aid of the Paraclete[4], and of offering up prayer in His Name[5]. Then, lifting up His eyes to heaven, in wrapt and solemn devotion, He committed the Apostles to the guardian care of the Eternal Father[6], and dedicated to Him His own completed work[7], which once more He contemplates in its issues not only on those then present, but on all that should believe on His Name[8]. After this solemn outpouring of His whole soul to God, which none can read or hear without feeling that nothing more sublime is recorded in the Book of Life, a hymn, probably the Hallel, was sung, and the Apostles went forth with their Lord to the Mount of Olives[9].

[1] Jn. xiv. 1—31.
[2] Jn. xv. 1—6.
[3] Jn. xv. 18—25.
[4] Jn. xvi. 1—16.
[5] Jn. xvi. 23—27.
[6] Jn. xvii.
[7] John xvii. 20.

[8] We can never fail to notice the strong sacrificial language now used by our Lord in the words, *and for their sakes I sanctify* (ἁγιάζω ἐμαυτον, i.e. *I consecrate Myself, I dedicate Myself to Thee in death*) that they may be consecrated through the truth, Jn. xiii. 19. Comp. ἁγιάζειν in LXX.; Levit. xxii. 2; Num. iii. 15. See Archbp. Trench's *N. T. Synonyms*, II. 168.

[9] Mtt. xxvi. 30; Mk. xiv. 26.

Such were the circumstances of the institution of a Rite, the uninterrupted celebration of which from the earliest times to the present day is an impregnable fact. Now (i) we find that in the Gospel narrative it occupies no isolated position. It is not only in complete harmony with, but is the culminating point of all previous announcements whether figurative or specific respecting the mystery of the Passion. Had the earliest explanation of the import of the Saviour's Name declared the *delivery of His people from their sins* to be the object of His coming into the world? We have here the remission of sins distinctly connected with His death. Had the Baptist, at the very commencement of his ministry, spoken of Him as *the Lamb of God that should take away the sin of the world*[1]? In the institution of the Eucharist, Bread and Wine, before subordinate and not even of Divine authority, are put in place of the lamb hitherto eaten, and of that victim itself no word is said. Had the Saviour at the first Passover of His public ministry, spoken of a mysterious *destruction* and *resurrection of His Body,* and declared that *as Moses lifted up the serpent in the wilderness, so must the Son of Man be lifted up?* He now embodies in a significant Rite the destruction of His Body, and its lifting up for the salvation of many. Had He, when another Paschal Festival came round, after one of His most significant miracles, spoken of Himself as the *Bread of Life,* of *eating His Body* and *drinking His Blood?* In this

[1] See Bp. Browne *on the Articles,* p. 711.

Rite not only is the same language recalled to the minds of His Apostles, not only is the same prominence given to the mysterious words *Body* and *Blood*, but the means, the *eating* and *drinking* then so incomprehensibly demanded and promised, are now actually supplied. Had the representatives of the Law and the Prophets conversed with the Saviour respecting *the decease He was about to accomplish at Jerusalem?* He now, at the greatest of the historical festivals of the Jews, embodies in a significant action the complete fulfilment of its typical ordinances in and through that decease. That previous training, which the brevity and conciseness of the narrative of the Institution renders absolutely necessary to explain its reception and celebration is supplied, and that so incidentally and undesignedly, in a manner so unmethodical and little studious about the disposition and arrangement of its parts, that we feel convinced of its truth and genuineness.

But, (ii), we have traced the institution of the Eucharist back to its source, to the only account of its origin which the Christian Churches have received, and beside which there is no vestige of any other. In an upper-room in the city of Jerusalem, the capital of one of the most despised kingdoms of the Roman empire, we have found a lowly Being surrounded by a few lowly followers, twelve men of sordid occupations, peasants, publicans, fishermen from Galilee, a district regarded as the lowest morally and socially even in Palestine itself. He is conscious that within a few short hours He will undergo the most ignominious punishment the Roman governor can inflict on the malefactor and the slave. This fact He has never disguised from His followers; it has formed the subject of frequent and earnest conversation. Calmly, deliberately, He has declared that He must undergo this death, that on it depends the most momentous issues alike to His disciples and the world at large. Though He has had no human soul, no relative, no friend, no disciple, with whom to take counsel in such a matter; though to His chosen disciples His words have been utterly unintelligible, yet He has never faltered when speaking of His death, and the consequences He has declared will flow from it[1]. Whenever He has spoken of them, it has never been in the heated language of the enthusiast or the fanatic. It has ever been calm, deliberate, majestic, simple. It has never betrayed a symptom of hesitation, but

[1] On the perfect self-reliance of the Saviour, see Ullmann's *Sinlessness of Jesus*, p. 70. E. T. 'Courage and faith are not unusual, when the principles that call them forth have been adopted by others, and have received this decisive proof of their adaptation and their truth. That which is true, indeed, is not more true by being understood and admitted, and what a man believes is not really more worthy of his belief than before, when it is accepted by others as well as himself. But mind leans on mind, nevertheless, and the enlightened convictions of one impart increased stability and strength to the enlightened convictions of another. What we could not effect or endure alone, we can effect and endure when supported by other kindred souls. Jesus knew no such support as this. He was followed by multitudes, but it was not because they understood and embraced His principles; and hence, when these principles were more fully disclosed, *many went back and walked no more with Him*, Jn. vi. 66.' Young's *Christ of History*, pp. 232, 3.

uniformly the composed and dignified *assurance*, the clear prescience of One who is perfectly aware of what is to be.

The 'hour' He has so often predicted is now nigh at hand, nay at the very door. But a few days back there was a moment when all Jerusalem was at His feet, when thousands were ready to welcome Him as the Messiah, and to exalt his triumph. That homage He accepted with the calm composure of one who felt it to be His due, but not for a single moment did He allow Himself to be drawn aside into any compliance with the popular expectations[1].

That one short hour of triumph has passed away never to return. He is now in a humble upper-room with His disciples. One of them, disappointed of the material prosperity he had promised himself by joining Him, filled with malice, has retired to mature a plan for delivering Him into the hands of the ruling powers, who have resolved on putting Him to death. Of this cruel treachery He is perfectly aware, nay, He has Himself indicated the traitor.

What, then, is His demeanour at this crisis? Does the calm composure of other hours forsake Him? Is there no hesitation, no misgiving *now?* Is there no fear of possible disappointment? At least, does He not request of His followers that they will conceal the fact of His disgraceful end?

So far from this, His language was never so calm,

[1] See Bp. Ellicott's *Lectures*, pp. 290, 1.

so unhesitating, so exalted above all human perplexity. Not only does He converse with His disciples respecting His end, but He institutes an Ordinance specially to *commemorate it for all future time*[1]*!* In the face of a cruel and ignominious death, at the season of one of the greatest of the Jewish festivals, He supersedes its ordinances, which have been celebrated from generation to generation, by another of His own appointment, declaring that *His Body is about to be broken, His Blood to be shed for many, for the remission of sins!* In the prospect of unutterable agony and shame He commends His chosen ones to the Divine protection, He prays that they may be kept from temptation; but of *Himself* He[2] speaks to the Supreme in words, the depth and breadth, and length, and height of which eighteen centuries have not fathomed, in words such as no mortal ever *has* or *could* address to the Author of his being, of a work He has accomplished, of commandments He has kept; though He has disappointed every earthly expectation, though He has achieved no abiding success whatsoever, He yet looks forward to His death as the very instrument of

[1] 'About to be crucified as a felon and a slave, He commanded and provided that the fact should be remembered to the end of time—did so in the full confidence that He should at last triumph. And the fact *has been* remembered. This is the mystery—if He be not all that He claimed to be—this is truly more miraculous than anything ever so called, more inexplicable on all natural principles.' Young's *Christ of History*, p. 238.

[2] On the sense of personal faultlessness and perfection ever exhibited by our Lord, see some striking remarks in Young's *Christ of History*, pp. 202—206; Ullmann, p. 95.

His triumph, and declares that by it and through it *He will draw all men unto Him!*

And that death He underwent! He suffered under Pontius Pilate! We need only state this article of the faith of the Universal Church. It is confirmed by heathen as well as Christian testimony. In four Gospels it is recorded with a minuteness the writers employ in treating of no other event in His life[1]. Heathen authors mention it as a matter of common notoriety; the opprobrious epithets applied to the early Christians presuppose it as a fact which admitted of no dispute; in an historical age, in a nation which had its archives, its registers, its monuments, which had the strongest possible interest in demonstrating the contrary, the fact was always accepted, *and never disproved.*

Where were His disciples when He died? One alone stood by His cross, one had denied with an oath that he had ever known Him, the rest had forsaken Him and fled. This is their own testimony. They do not hide or disguise it. With singular openness and artless minuteness they describe their own cowardice and faithlessness!

We may conclude, then, that they now went back to their homes. They had given up everything to follow their Master; they had gone after Him, as thousands did after other Messiahs, but they had been disappointed, and they tried to forget all that had occurred, to efface all recollection of their mistake?

[1] For some remarks on the fulness of detail in the Evangelic accounts of the Passion, see Thomson's *Bampton Lectures*, pp. 101, 2.

On the contrary, little more than forty days afterwards, they were to be found at Jerusalem[1], where they elected not in a covert underhand manner, but openly and fearlessly, even by lot, another Apostle to fill up their original number[2]. Ten days after this, one of the Apostles, and he no other than the very Peter, who scarcely a year before could not endure the idea of his Master's death, who had in a moment of temptation thrice denied that he had ever known Him, stood forth in Jerusalem, in the very place where His Master had been crucified, to declare that though He had died, He was yet the Messiah whom the prophets had predicted, whom the nation was looking for, whom God had promised[3]. Nay, the effect of his words was such that three thousand[4] men did not hesitate to avow their belief in the crucified One as the Messiah, in spite of the shame of the Cross to submit to Baptism into His name, to form themselves into a society based on a belief in Him, and dissociating themselves from the strongly-rooted prejudices of their childhood, their country, and their age, to teach that all sacrificial observances had been once and for ever fulfilled

[1] 'In the heart of that city where the people would be most exasperated at the revival of the sect which they had supposed to have perished with its Founder; where there would be the greatest disinclination to believe, and the greatest solicitude to confute; where the counter-proofs were in the hands of their enemies; where all the people, high and low, had been committed in the transaction, and to whom the preaching Christ not merely abased their national pride, but reproached them with most odious national cruelty.' Milman, *Bampton Lectures*, p. 86.

[2] Acts i. 22. [3] Acts ii. 14—36. [4] Acts ii. 41.

by the death of One, whom fifty days before they had seen suspended on a cross between two thieves!

Now of these extraordinary facts there is only one adequate and consistent explanation, even that which all the disciples in spite of obloquy, contempt, and persecution made it the business of their lives to proclaim, which every extant letter they wrote[1], and every treatise that Christian authors have since composed, assumes, *the Resurrection of Jesus Christ from the dead.*

The Evangelists inform us that a few hours after the last High-priestly prayer had been offered up in the upper-room at Jerusalem, and after a final and mysterious Conflict in the garden of Gethsemane[2], the Saviour was delivered into the hands of men. All that He had solemnly foretold to His disciples came to pass. He was mocked, He was buffeted, He was spitted on,

[1] See *Restoration of Belief*, and Dean Goodwin's *Hulsean Lectures*, p. 42.

[2] It has been well observed that the Agony is on human principles wholly misplaced; 'it comes before the time, when as yet there is no arrest; and no human prospect that there will be any. The Saviour is at large to go where He pleases, and is in perfect outward safety.' See Bushnell's *Nature and the Supernatural*, p. 39; *Aids to Faith*, p. 360. 'The narrative of the Agony,' remarks Lange, *Life of Christ*, IV. 270, 'guarantees its authenticity by its enigmatically mysterious nature. It is a representation which lies beyond the mental capacity of ordinary human or Christian invention. It belongs to those portions which the Church, in all its weak moods, members, and theologians, most of all in its weak critics, would have in many ways surrendered, because of its presumed offences, and which it has only preserved in consequence of its motives, namely, its historical faithfulness in the transmission of this history.'

He was scourged, He was nailed to the Cross, and after a final and mysterious cry *It is finished*[1], He bowed his head and died, at which moment the beautiful Veil[2] that separated the Holy Place from the most Holy in the Temple was rent in twain from the top to the bottom[3], and the earth shook, and the rocks were rent, and the graves were opened.

The Holy Body, continues the Gospel narrative, was taken down from the Cross, and laid, not, as a writer anxious only to exalt the Apostolic band would assuredly have related, by any of the Apostles, but by secret disciples and comparative strangers in a new tomb. There, the stone sealed and the watch set, it lay till the morning of the first day of the week, when the women who had gone thither to complete the process of embalming, found the stone rolled away, and the sepulchre empty!

They had hardly time to recover from their astonishment, and to run with the announcement to the disciples, when the risen Saviour appeared to Mary

1 None can fail to notice the complete harmony of these words with all that the Saviour had said during His life of a *work He had to accomplish.* Could such minute coincidences as these have been preserved by any human *idealist?*

2 Matt. xxvii. 51; Mk. xv. 38; Lk. xxiii. 45.

3 We are often told that in forming an opinion of the true character of the death of Christ, we must *rest on the Gospels, and not import into them the language and figures of the Epistles.* Now it is worth remarking, that this rending of the Veil is related *only in the Gospels.* Had this appeared in the course of an argument in one of the Epistles, in that, for instance, to the Hebrews, we should have been told perhaps that it was merely a Jewish figure, perhaps that 'it was a later insertion to justify the reference.'

Magdalene[1], and not to her only, but on the same day to Peter[2], during the afternoon to the two disciples journeying towards Emmaus[3], in the evening to the ten in the absence of Thomas[4], and seven days afterwards to the same body when that Apostle was present[5]. During forty days after His Resurrection He continued to manifest Himself to them from time to time; to the seven on the lake of Gennesareth[6]; to five hundred brethren at once, the majority of whom were alive twenty years afterwards[7]; to James[8]; then once more to all the Apostles.

There was, indeed, a mystery about the risen Body. Before, the Apostles had been aware of the place of their Lord's abode, of His going out and His coming in. But now there is a change. He comes they know not whence, He goes they know not whither, and only from time to time does He reveal Himself to them.

But by many infallible proofs they were assured of His Resurrection. 'It was not one person but many who saw Him; they saw Him not only separately but together; not by night only but by day; not at a distance but near; not once, but several times; they not only saw Him, but touched Him, conversed with Him,

[1] Matt. xxviii. 9, 10.
[2] Lk. xxiv. 34; 1 Cor. xv. 6.
[3] Lk. xxiv. 13—25.
[4] Jn. xx. 19—25; Lk. xxiv. 36—43.
[5] Jn. xx. 26—29. [6] Jn. xxi. 1—24. [7] 1 Cor. xv. 7.
[8] 1 Cor. xv. 7. For an able summary of all that has been written on the appearances after the Resurrection, see Andrews, 492—513.

ate with Him, examined His Person to satisfy their doubts[1].'

And at length, after He had once and again conversed with them, on the complete fulfilment in Himself of all things written in the Law of Moses and in the Psalms and in the Prophets, *opening their understandings that they might understand the Scriptures*[2], and commissioning them *to preach the Gospel to every creature,* He led them forth to Bethany, and lifting up His hands He blessed them, and it came to pass, while He was in the act of blessing them, *He was parted from them, and a cloud received Him out of their sight*[3].

Such is the unanimous testimony of the four Evangelists, such was the unanimous belief of all the Apostles, who had the best means of knowing the truth; who, without a particle of worldly interest in the matter, voluntarily exposed themselves to labours, dangers, and sufferings in proclaiming this account. The Resurrection is not an event incidentally noticed in one or two early Christian writings, it is the very ground and foundation of the Apostolic preaching[4], it is asserted or assumed in every Christian writing we possess, and

[1] Paley's *Evidences*. [2] Lk. xxiv. 26, 27, 44, 45.

[3] Lk. xxiv. 50; Acts i. 9.

[4] *If Christ*, says St Paul to the Corinthians, *be not raised, your faith is vain, ye are yet in your sins*, 1 Cor. xv. 17. 'By our Lord's resurrection we may be *assured* concerning the *efficacy* of His undertakings for us; for considering it we may not doubt of God's being reconciled to us,' Barrow's *Sermon on the Resurrection*, in Wordsworth's *Institutes*, II. 267; Pearson, *On the Creed;* Baxter's *Catechism*, in Wordsworth, I. 299.

in an age which had more interest than any other in so doing, it was *never disproved.*

If it did not take place, then we are called upon to believe that the Apostles, who had been trained in sacrificial habits, who from early associations, from the force of habit, and all those influences which are so potent with mankind, would naturally have been disposed to exalt the sacrificial system[1], without any adequate assignable reason declared it to be done away, and ascribed to a 'crucified Man, Divine predicates which stood in direct contradiction with Jewish monotheism[2],' though for such ascription they had no real ground whatever! We are called upon to believe that the Apostles, who till the last moment could not realize to themselves that their Lord would die; who, whenever He spake to them on the subject, did not understand His words; who, on the day He did die were by their own confession scattered abroad as sheep, every hope buried in His grave, yet within fifty days after that event could be transformed into new men, from being weak and cowardly could become bold and

[1] 'Think what it was to the Jew in the Apostolical age, to see his religion with all its far-back memories and associations *vanishing away*... we know what a spell the religion of their fathers had for thousands in Israel, how it rallied the bloodthirsty ruffians of the final siege round the ruins of the burning sanctuary...how it awakened a glow of patriotic enthusiasm in the breast even of the renegade Josephus while he described his descent from the house of Levi...what (outwardly at least) had their new faith to give its votaries in compensation for the loss of recollections so august, of institutions so sacred?' Dean Stanley's *Sermons on the Apostolical Age*, p. 354.

[2] Dorner's *Person of Christ*, Vol. I. p. 47. E. T.

outspoken; could stand up in the very place where their Master had suffered, to proclaim an *idea*, a *fancy* of their own that He was risen from the dead[1]! We are called upon to believe that in an age, when neither civilization nor philosophy had eradicated or simplified the ancient sacrificial system; when men were exhausting themselves in the ardour of inventing some fresh superstition, when they were commonly addicted to cruel and revolting ceremonies[2]; out of the very centre of Judaism, out of a system penetrated with sacrificial habits emerged a body of men to teach that all sacrificial observance had been done away through the death of a crucified Man, who during His life on earth

[1] 'The supposition that the Apostles were deceivers is utterly absurd. Let us follow it out: imagine these twelve men assembled together after the death of Christ, contriving a scheme to represent Him, falsely, as raised from the dead. The human heart is strangely addicted to levity and change, and warped by hopes and benefits. Let only one out of the number have been dazzled by these attractions; and others of them, again, terrified by imprisonment, tortures, and death; their plot would have been ruined! Follow out this, I say.' Pascal, *Works*, Vol. III. p. 310. See also Milman's *Bampton Lectures*, 51, 52.

[2] On the strange gods and still stranger rites introduced during the later period of the Roman Empire, see Döllinger, *Jew and Gentile*, II. 173—178. The horrible Taurobolium, it will be remembered, was resorted to not only for individual purification, but for the welfare of others, and particularly the Emperor and the imperial family. 'A roomy grave was dug, and covered with pierced boards; the victim, a bull or ram, was sacrificed on these, so that the blood dropped through the holes like rain, and was caught by the man below on his whole body, a ceremony supposed to effect a complete purification for twenty years.' See *Prudentii Peristephanon*, 1036—1040; 1046—1050;

Quin os supinat, obvias offert genas
Supponit aures, labra, nares objicit,
Oculos et ipsos perluit liquoribus:

had achieved no complete success, and of whom after His death, they could give no account save an enthusiastic idea that He had risen! Nay more, we are called upon to believe that they not only proclaimed this idea, but succeeded in persuading[1] men of its truth, banished into oblivion the ten thousand sacrifices of *various nations*, and in place of a ritual hallowed by the memories of ages, substituted a Rite to the outward senses of the most mysterious simplicity, and commemorating nothing more than a cruel and ignominious death!

We need not ask if such an opinion can be entertained even for a moment.

The early celebration of the Eucharist, whether we consider the period at which it began, or the persons who first celebrated it, or the immense importance then attached to sacrificial observances[2], remains and ever

Nec jam palato parcit, et linguam rigat,
Donec cruorem totus atrum conbibat

....

Huc inquinatum talibus contagiis
Tabo recentis sordidum piaculi
Omnes salutant atque adorant eminus
Vilis quod illum sanguis et bos mortuus
Fœdis latentem sub cavernis laverint.

[1] Though it is 'the rarest of phenomena to find *any* religion which is capable of transcending the limits of race, clime, and the scene of its historic origin; a religion which, if transplanted, will not die; a religion which is more than a local or national growth of superstition!' Rogers' *Reason and Faith*, p. 37.

[2] Though after the destruction of Jerusalem Jewish sacrificial observances gradually disappeared, yet 'the study and exposition of the laws of the Temple and of sacrifice were the principal compensations,' as it was believed that these laws *were speedily to become available again;* nay, 'it was decreed that a priest was not to drink wine on the day he would have been on duty at the Temple, had

must remain an 'insoluble phenomenon,' except by the admission of the fact of the Resurrection. This affords a satisfactory account of the matter, and 'no other satisfactory account can be given, nor any account at all, but what is imaginary merely and invented[1].'

Once grant that HE, whose marvellous life the Gospel narrative records, was, as He claimed to be, as He is there represented, and as He has been acknowledged by multitudes of all nations and tongues, of all classes and conditions, perfect Man and perfect God; grant that gathering up again the human race in Himself, as the true Paschal Lamb He put away the sin of the world, that He rose again on the third day, and ascended up on high as the true High Priest of our redeemed humanity; and we can understand how in spite of the shame of the Cross the old sacrificial language concentrated around His person and work; we can understand how the ancient sacrificial ritual which prevailed so universally down to the period of His death, then as universally began to disappear; we can understand how the first observers of the Eucharist were assured of the acceptance of the sacrifice therein symbolized and shewn forth; we can understand how the death commemorated in that Rite could be regarded by them not only as a propitiatory sacrifice, but one which, in a far higher

its regulations still continued in force, for the miracle of the restoration might take place on that very day, and according to the law the priest ought to be fasting then: and *proselytes were to deposit a sum of money, that the legal sacrifice might be bought with it, in case of the restoration of the Temple.*' Döllinger's *Gentile and Jew*, II. 415.

[1] Butler's *Analogy*, Pt. II. Ch. VI.

and more efficacious degree than they had ever known before, realized to them that pardon and reconciliation which was the aim of the ancient sacrificial ritual; and lastly, we can discern causes powerful enough to have produced the most wonderful revolution in the religious history of mankind that the world has seen[1], and which has subsisted to the present day.

On any other hypothesis, the religious history of mankind presents us for upwards of four thousand years with a long, waste, purposeless parenthesis of useless rites and ceremonies; Judaism had no substance of which it was the shadow; heathenism had no reality after which its ten thousand sacrifices were a confused outcry; the whole history of the world is naught else than an insoluble enigma, 'an inextricable labyrinth, a huge pile of blocks and fragments of an unfinished edifice, and the great tragedy of humanity remains devoid of all proper result[2].'

[1] Εἰ χρὴ καὶ τῷ εἰκότι χρῆσθαι λόγῳ περὶ τῆς ἀρχῆθεν Χριστιανῶν συστάσεως, φήσομεν ὅτι οὐ πιθανὸν...τοὺς ἀκροωμένους [τῶν Ἀποστόλων] μετατεθεῖσθαι ἐκ πατρίων πολυχρονίων ἐθῶν, μὴ ἀξιολόγου τινὸς δυνάμεως αὐτοὺς καὶ τεραστίων πραγμάτων μετακινησάντων ἐπὶ τὰ οὕτω ξένα καὶ ἀλλότρια τῶν συντρόφων αὐτοῖς δογμάτων. Origen. c. *Celsum*, VIII. 47.

[2] Schlegel's *Philosophy of History*.

CHAPTER VIII.

THE EUCHARIST A SACRIFICIAL FEAST.

Οὐ δύνασθε ποτήριον Κυρίου πίνειν καὶ ποτήριον δαιμονίων· οὐ δύνασθε τραπέζης Κυρίου μετέχειν καὶ τραπέζης δαιμονίων.

S. PAUL, 1 *Cor.* x. 21.

AND now that we have seen in the institution and early celebration of the Lord's Supper one of the strongest evidences of the truth of the Gospel Narrative, of the reality of the Incarnation, Death, Resurrection, and Ascension of our Lord as therein set forth, we would advance a step further, and regard it also as an evidence of the Christian doctrine of the Atonement.

Much, indeed, of what might be said upon this point has been already anticipated, but several particulars still remain for consideration.

i. The Sacrament of the Lord's Supper under its first and most obvious aspect presupposes the propitiatory effect of the sufferings and death of Christ. This view has never been wanting in any age of Christianity, and the early and general celebration of this Rite in a sacrificial age by multitudes who had from their earliest years been brought up in sacrificial habits, is a decisive proof that they understood the Death therein commemorated, not as a mere martyrdom, but as a true sacrifice, similar to, though far surpassing the expiatory sacrifices with which they had been so long familiar.

For, if the Death of Christ was merely a corroboration of His teaching, if it was merely the greatest moral act done in the world, if it was merely a martyrdom, the greatest of all martyrdoms in the cause of Divine truth, then, how comes it to pass that neither the Apostles, nor the early Christians, either revised, rearranged or reimposed on their converts the ancient sacrificial system? If the Eucharist was simply a memorial of His Death, what adequate reason can be assigned for the cessation of the ancient sacrificial ritual? Why should not these sacrifices in some modified form have been continued, at least amongst Gentile nations[1]? From the earliest times, as we have seen, they had been celebrated for a most real and definite purpose. From the earliest times they had been deemed to be in some mysterious manner capable of making good man's imperfect consecration of himself

[1] The destruction of the Temple naturally put an end to all sacrifices *amongst the Jews*, so closely were they bound up with the temple and its altar; 'for, according to the universal teaching of the Rabbies, all private sacrifices were for ever illegal, from the time Solomon's Temple was dedicated. Later on, too, teachers of note declared that every one who sacrificed without the Temple ought to be punished with "cutting off." Even the use of serving roasted meat on the evening of the Passover, as a feeble remembrance of the former sacrificial repast on that day, was reprobated by the more scrupulous Jews.' Döllinger, II. 415.

to God. This feeling was never stronger than at the time when the celebration of the Eucharist began, and no men since the world began ever held deeper views of the extreme heinousness of sin, and of the necessity of some atonement over and above mere repentance, than those who first celebrated this Rite. And yet they never readjusted or reimposed the ancient sacrificial ritual even in the most modified form, but uniformly spake of it as 'fulfilled' and 'done away'! These are the facts of the case, and the idea that Christ died as a martyr in the cause of truth does not explain them, it does not account for the *total and overmastering change* of thought and feeling in respect to sacrificial observances which has invariably accompanied the reception and celebration of the Lord's Supper.

ii. But, again, so far is this view of Christ's Death from accounting for this extraordinary change which is a matter of history, that it does not even explain the institution of the Rite itself.

For let us allow for a moment that the Saviour's Death was merely a corroboration of His teaching, that He suffered as a martyr, the greatest of all martyrs; let us imagine that His disciples wished, from feelings of deep affection and reverence, to commemorate His Death; then it is conceivable that this end would have been attained by a moving recital from time to time of its tender and touching circumstances. Or we may go further, and imagine that they might have met to break bread and to pour out wine, as a symbolical representation of His Body broken and His Blood poured out. But even granting this, in spite of its extreme improbability, considering *the religious importance* which *as Jews* they attached to the idea of breaking bread and pouring out wine[1] even at a common meal, what explanation is to be given of the *partaking* of these symbols by those who celebrated this Rite? What point of connection is there between such a ceremonial and the commemoration of a mere martyrdom, though the martyr had been the holiest man that ever lived? And how comes it to pass that there never has existed a similar mode of commemorating the death of any other martyr? The very character, therefore, of the ordinance of the Eucharist, the very form in which it is celebrated is unaccountable on the supposition that our Lord's Death was no more than a martyrdom, or an eminent sacrifice to the cause of truth[2].

iii. But the argument is immeasurably strengthened by the slightest consideration of the words of our Lord at the institution of the Eucharist, the time when they were uttered, and the persons to whom they were addressed.

For when He took the Bread, and blessed and brake it, He not only said, *Take, eat, this is My Body*, but He added, *which is for you, which is given* [broken]

[1] 'There were Jewish ascetics, who, in memory of the sacrificial import of partaking of meat and wine, wholly abstained from both after the destruction of the Temple of Jerusalem. "Shall we eat flesh," said they, "which was once offered in the sacrifice that now has ceased? Shall we drink wine, of which drink-offerings used to be prepared, but is now no longer?"' Döllinger's *Gentile and Jew*, II. p. 416, and refs.

[2] See Archbp. Whately *on the Sacraments*, p. 106.

for you. Again, when He took the cup, He not only said, *Drink ye all of this*, but, *This cup is the New Covenant in My Blood, which is shed for you, for many for the remission of sins.*

Now we have already seen how completely the language here employed is in harmony with all He had ever said before, whether privately to His Apostles, or publicly to the Jews, respecting the purpose of His Death. But the solemnity of the occasion, when this Rite was instituted, utterly precludes the idea that the language here employed can be explained away, as a mere rhetorical use of Jewish figures. It was no multitude that He was addressing, it was no knot of unbelievers with whom He was reclining at the table, whose prejudices it was necessary to soothe, whose feelings it was necessary to consult. They were the companions of His early ministry, the men whom He had been pleased to call out of the world to be the heralds of His Gospel, whom in His infinite condescension He had called 'His friends,' whom He had endeared to Himself by many acts of kindness, by loving counsels, and mysterious sympathy, and who had given up everything to follow Him.

Was it a time, then, for mere rhetorical figures? Were they the men to whom He was likely to speak in language adapted merely to their Jewish prejudices? The words even of common men and women are earnest and real, when they are conscious that death is drawing nigh; can we possibly conceive this to be less true of HIM, who was emphatically THE TRUTH?

On an occasion, then, of such inconceivable solemnity He instituted this sacred Feast, not simply in commemoration of Himself, but of Himself in a particular character, as about to give *His Body for them*, as about to *shed His Blood for them*, and *for many*, and that *for the remission of sins*[1]. These are not the words of St Paul, St Peter, or St John, or of the author of the Epistle to the Hebrews. They are the words of Him who delivered the Sermon on the Mount; who therein declared that He had not come to 'destroy the Law, but to fulfil it;' who fulfilled its moral requirements by deepening them, by developing principles as lying beneath enactments, the spirit beneath the letter; who, on one memorable occasion, bade certain objectors go and learn what one of their own prophets had meant, when he said that the Lord would *have mercy and not sacrifice*[2]; who inveighed in awful and earnest words against 'the leaven of the Pharisees[3],' against making the Law void through the traditions of men[4]; the echoes of whose lofty morality are even now reverberating through the length and breadth of Christendom, passing into laws, into proverbs, into principles of social life, yet 'never passing

1 'We must consider,' remarks Warburton, 'not only what Jesus said now, but what He said and did; and not only that, but the *mode* of saying and doing; relative to the time, the occasion, the manners, and the customs of the age; otherwise the Speaker's meaning can be but very imperfectly understood without taking in all these things.' Warburton, *Wks.* v. 552.

2 Hosea vi. 6; Matt. xii. 7; ix. 13.

3 Matt. xvi. 6; Lk. xii. 1.

4 Matt. xv. 6; Mk. vii. 9.

away,' ever presenting some new, some deeper truth, to the successive generations of the sons of men.

But on this momentous occasion it is not in the language of the moralist that He addresses His chosen Twelve. It is in *sacrificial* language, and in *sacrificial* terms that He speaks to them for the last time of the event about to occur to Himself. They who heard Him were men not only of a peculiar religious education, but of an education based on sacrifice, and that to an extent we can hardly conceive[1]. With them no morning dawned, no evening closed, no harvest was housed, no vintage was gathered in, no sin of omission was expiated, no ceremonial impurity was removed without the intervention of sacrifice in some form or other. From generation to generation their fathers and their fathers' fathers had been trained never to conceive of the remission of sins otherwise than through the mediation of sacrifice. What other ideas, then, when they heard now, or when they reflected afterwards, on the words that accompanied the institution of the Eucharist, could have been suggested to the minds of the Apostles, but those of an atoning sacrifice, of a death to be undergone for them, and for their eternal benefit? Surely if these words, so solemn andso mo mentous, were not designed to suggest the ideas they would of necessity evoke, we may believe that HE, who was *The Truth,* would have guarded them by some explanation, and would have prevented their being thus misunder-

[1] See Dean Goodwin's *Hulsean Lectures*, p. 26.

stood. But as though, like seeds, they were to fall on a soil ready prepared to receive them, as though they were the key which would obviously reveal the cypher, they are uttered with solemn and significant action, but no lengthened explanation is vouchsafed[1].

But this is not all. The Saviour speaks of His Blood as the Blood of 'the New Covenant.' Now as addressed to the Apostles, the very word *Covenant* implied the idea of a sacrifice ratifying and attesting it, and not only of a sacrifice, but of a *feast upon a sacrifice.* To whatever *covenant* their thoughts then or afterwards carried them back, whether to that ratified with their great forefather Abraham[2], or to that which 'amidst thunderings and voices and the noise of a trumpet' Jehovah made with the emancipated nation at Sinai[3], the accompanying sacrifices could not have been forgotten.

On the memorable occasion, indeed, last alluded to, the Jewish Lawgiver, after building an altar at the foot of the Mount and setting up twelve stones of memorial, caused calves and goats to be slain as burnt-offerings and peace-offerings, and sprinkled one-half of the blood on the altar and the roll containing the covenant-condi-

[1] 'It appeareth by many examples, that the Apostles of their own disposition were very scrupulous and inquisitive, yea, in other cases, of less importance and difficulty, always apt to move questions. How cometh it to pass, that so few words of so high a mystery being uttered, they receive with gladness the gift of Christ, and make no show of doubt or scruple.' Hooker, *Eccl. Pol.* Bk. v. See also Pelling's *Discourse on the Lord's Supper*, London, 1685.

[2] Gen. xv. 8—12.

[3] Ex. xxiv. 3—9.

tions, and the other half upon the people, saying, *Behold the blood of the Covenant which the Lord hath made with you concerning all these words*[1]. And when this ceremony was ended, Aaron and his sons Nadab and Abihu, and seventy elders, as representatives of the people, ascended to a level spot near the summit of the mountain[2], and there partook of the Covenant Feast, thus, in conformity with the constant practice of antiquity, receiving the seal and pledge of the alliance which had just been concluded.

Now they, to whom our Lord was speaking, were made perfectly familiar not only by these solemn associations, but by every celebration of a peace-offering, and especially of the Passover, in which the idea of the peace-offering found its highest expression, with the conception of a feast upon a sacrifice. Uttered in their hearing, the words *This is My Blood of the New Covenant* could not fail to be understood as implying that, as in the old Dispensation God had made covenant with Israel with the blood of beasts, so the New Feast instituted by Him, who was about 'to give His life a ransom for many,' was a feast upon a sacrifice, ratifying

[1] Ex. xxxv. 8. Compare Jeremiah xxxi. 31—34.

[2] Ex. xxiv. 11. 'Tantum abfuit ut mortui errent, ut convivium sacrificiale hilares celebraverint.' Rosenmüller, *in loc.* Outram, *de Sacrificiis*, I. v. 5. See O. Von Gerlach *on the Pentateuch*, p. 308. Cudworth, *de Cœnâ Domini*, Chap. I. sect. 2. 'Certe non in hoc tantum sed et in Baptismi Sacramento videtur omnino Christus se non Hebræorum tantum sed et Gentium in idem fœdus cooptandarum captui accommodasse.' Grotius in Matt. xxvi. 27.

a new and better covenant between the Lord and His people[1].

iv. That the Rite thus instituted was regarded as a feast upon a sacrifice by the first Christians, who being trained under a sacrificial system were far more likely to interpret it aright than ourselves at this distance of time, is furnished by the language of the Apostle Paul, who was the first to apply to it the name of the *Lord's Supper,* and the only one of the Apostolic body who has treated of its celebration.

The testimony, indeed, of this Apostle is of the utmost conceivable importance. For not only had he been trained in Judaism, but he had belonged to one of the very strictest of its sects, he had been brought up at the feet of one of its most learned and eminent teachers. No one, therefore, could be more truly a representative of the ideas of his nation, no one could more adequately express the feelings, with which in a sacrificial age the early Christians joined in the celebration of this Rite.

This testimony he delivers in a letter written about the year A.D. 57, the authenticity of which has never been disputed, and which even the most recent scepticism accepts as genuine.

Now in this letter we not only have the earliest record of the institution of the Eucharist, but we have a proof that within a very short time after the Ascen-

[1] Bp. Browne *on the Articles,* p. 716. Freeman's *Principles of Divine Service,* II. 3.

sion, wherever the Christian Church was established, there in place of the sacrifices, to which the early Christians, whether Jews or Gentiles, were accustomed, this Rite and this only was celebrated, which in any way approximated to the ancient sacrificial ideas. As we read the Apostle's words, we can almost recall the very manner in which this Rite was celebrated at this very early period. 'We almost see the banquet spread in the late evening, after the sun had set behind the western ridge of the hills of Achaia; we see the many torches blazing as at Troas[1], to light up the darkness of the upper-room, where, as was their wont, the Christian community assembled; we see the couches laid and the walls hung, after the manner of the East, as on the night of the betrayal[2];' we see the rich 'of their abundance' and the poor 'of their poverty' contributing to the Agape, the social meal which then formed the preliminary of the sacred Feast; we see at its conclusion the bread broken, and the wine poured out, and we hear the institutional words pronounced as first they fell upon the Apostles' ears, and as the writer of this letter himself had heard them by direct revelation from his ascended Lord[3].

But over and above this there is far more to engage our attention.

One of the questions on which the Apostle had been consulted concerned a matter of the strongest interest

[1] Λαμπάδες ἱκαναί, Acts xx. 8.

[2] Dean Stanley's *Commentary on the Corinthians*, 1 Cor. xi. 1.

[3] 1 Cor. xi. 23.

to the early Christian community, viz. whether it was lawful for Christians to join in the heathen sacrificial feasts. At Corinth, as in all Greek towns, as indeed throughout the whole ancient world, the connection between a sacrifice and a feast was of the closest possible character[1]. Most public entertainments, and nearly all private meals, were more or less remotely connected with sacrifice. The difficulty, therefore, of avoiding contamination with idol feasts was proportionately great.

How, then, does the Apostle advise the Corinthians in this matter? As he is dictating the words of his reply to his amanuensis in some obscure quarter of the great city of Ephesus, let us pause for a moment to realize the scenes amidst which he was living. Ephesus was then the very centre and focus of idolatrous worship. At the head of its harbour was the great temple of Diana or Artemis, the magnificence of which was a proverb throughout the civilized world, as also the devotion of the city to its tutelary divinity. What Jerusalem was to the Christian pilgrim of the Middle

[1] See Cudworth's *True Notion*, Chap. I. 'These hallowed banquets formed the principal object of, and most effective bonds of union in, religious associations; and hence meal-time and sacrifice were so essentially connected together, that even the modes of expressing the two acts were frequently interchanged.' Döllinger's *Gentile and Jew*, I. 233; II. 84. 'Nullum fere Sacrificium sine aliquo epulo, et vicissim nullum pæne epulum, etiam profanum, publicum præsertim, sine sacris quibusdam ritibus atque cæremoniis fuit celebratum. Quum ipsa quoque Sacrificia quid fuerunt aliud quam quædam quasi epulæ atque convivia, secundum illud Poetæ

...epulis accumbere Divum?'

Stuckius, *Sacrific. Sacror. Descrip.*

Ages, or Mecca to the Mohametan, or Benares to the Hindu, that was Ephesus to all the cities of Ionia, and indeed to the whole world. Go where he would, the eye of the Apostle rested on the offering of sacrifices before every temple and at every shrine. Go where he would, he saw the stricken victim yielding up its life, a portion laid upon the altar, and the rest given up to the sacrificers to supply materials for a sacrificial feast. The same rites were enacted in every city, every town, every village throughout the Roman world; from wellnigh every mountain and every hill the steam of sacrifice ascended up to heaven.

Amidst scenes like these, then, consecrated in the minds of men by the associations of centuries, the cessation of which would have been deemed utterly beyond all bounds of possibility, and the very conception of it a mark of madness, the Apostle dictates his advice to the Corinthian Christians respecting their attendance at the idol feast.

How, then, does he proceed? He reminds them of *the true nature and the surpassing dignity and solemnity* of the Eucharistic feast, saying,

My dearly beloved, flee from idolatry. I speak as to wise men, judge ye what I say. The Cup of Blessing which we bless, is it not the communion of the Blood of Christ? The Bread which we break, is it not the communion of the Body of Christ? For we being many are one bread and one body: for we are all partakers of that one bread. Behold Israel after the flesh: are not they which eat of the sacrifices partakers of the altar? What say I then? that the idol is any thing, or that which is offered in sacrifice to idols is anything? But I say, that the things which the Gentiles sacrifice, they sacrifice to demons, and not to God: and I would not that ye should have fellowship with demons. Ye cannot drink the cup of the Lord and the cup of demons: ye cannot be partakers of the Lord's Table and of the table of demons[1].

Now the first point deserving of attention here is the claim of the Apostle to be speaking to *wise men: I speak unto wise men, judge ye what I say.* 'Whence,' remarks Bp. Warburton[2], 'we may fairly conclude the reasoning to be such as *wise men* would not disdain to consider, and so regularly conducted as *wise men* would best comprehend. In a word, pursued with that science and precision which leaves no room for a loose, popular, and inaccurate interpretation.'

But, secondly, in this argument addressed to wise men, by one eminent above his equals for his acquaintance with Judaism, he assumes a perfect analogy between Jewish, Pagan and Christian sacrifices, and that *they are all parallels to one another.* 'If the three feasts, Jewish, Pagan and Christian,' remarks the same eminent authority we have just quoted[3], 'had not one

[1] 1 Cor. x. 14—21. Hence afterwards the charge of the heathens against the Christians that they did *Præcerptos cibos et delibatos altaribus potus abhorrere,* Minucius Felix, XII. 5.

[2] *Wks.* Vol. v. p. 549.

[3] *Wks.* Vol. v. p. 550. It has also been noticed that the fact of the Eucharist being a Sacrificial Feast is one of the reasons why we find so few directions in the New Testament about preparation for a worthy reception of it. 'There is little, or nothing said upon this subject, setting aside what St Paul once occasionally said of self-examination in

common nature, how could the apostle have inferred that this intercommunity was absolutely inconsistent?... For though there might be *Impiety* in the promiscuous use of Pagan and Christian rites, yet the *Inconsistency* arises from their having a common nature; and so, consequently (as they had opposite originals), from their destroying one another's effects, in the very celebration. The reasoning stands thus. Those who eat of the sacrifices were partakers of the altar. A sacrifice at the altar was a *Federal* Rite: consequently a feast upon that sacrifice became a Federal Rite likewise. The Lord's Table, and the table of devils, therefore, being both federal Rites, the same man could not be partaker of both. This is the Apostle's argument to the *wise men* here appealed to: and we see it turns altogether on this postulatum, that the Lord's Supper is of the nature of *a feast upon the sacrifice.* Suppose it now *a general commemoration only of a dead benefactor,* and all this reasoning vanishes; for though a man cannot execute

1 Cor. xi. 28. For the thing was not so very needful; because such directions might easily be drawn even from the consideration of the nature and uses of this Holy Banquet, and men already had great impressions and apprehensions of their duty in order to a due celebration of those solemnities, to which this mystery was parallel and analogous. With what religion did the very heathens prepare themselves, by washing their bodies, and by abstaining from worldly and carnal pleasures, before they addressed themselves to the tables of their gods? And with what care and curiosity did the Jews pick every crumb of leaven out of their houses, and use other observances, before they presumed to eat of the Passover? The very resemblance and analogy between this mystery and that is enough to minister directions about preparing and purifying our spirits in order to it.' Pelling *on the Lord's Supper,* p. 28. London, 1685.

two federal Rites which destroy one another, yet a *federal rite* and a *bare remembrance,* in two contrary religions, have none of this opposition; but may be celebrated, if not without *impiety*, yet without any of that *inconsistency* which the learned Apostle here charges upon his licentious Corinthians.'

It is clear, then, that the Apostle regarded the Lord's Supper in the light of a feast upon a sacrifice, and it is inconceivable that he could have so regarded it had the Death of the Saviour been merely that of a martyr. With the idea of a feast upon a sacrifice he and the early Christians were familiar[1]. With the idea of a solemn meal commemorating a martyrdom, or the death of any saint, however eminent, Abraham, or Moses, or David, they had been made familiar by no single event, type, symbol, or ceremonial of that Economy

[1] 'The Jews of our Saviour's age spoke the same language that He spoke: He had read their sacred books: He had submitted to their laws: their manners and customs were familiar to Him; the objects, about which He was conversant, natural, moral, religious and political, were continually presented to their minds also. If we, by deliberately comparing different parts of the New and Old Testament with one another, are sometimes enabled to discover His meaning, when they comprehended it but imperfectly, it *would more frequently happen that His countrymen and contemporaries would see the full force of His words*, when they are not so fully understood by us. We are not to appeal to the Jews of His time, as the best judges of the truth of His doctrines; but we may confidently appeal to them as competent *interpreters of words* spoken in their own language, addressed to them, intended first for their information, and next, for that of the whole world. Of the meaning of these words, our Saviour's contemporaries and countrymen were unquestionably the best judges.' Wilson's *Explanation of the New Testament*, p. 99.

under which they had lived. That 'full efflorescence of sacrificial thought and language with' which, as we have seen, the Apostle could speak of the Eucharist, is perfectly intelligible, if we recognise in our Lord's institution a real sacrificial action, and in the ordinance He instituted in place of the ancient Paschal Meal, an analogous though infinitely higher Passover commemorating a sacrifice for a deliverance from sin. On any other supposition, it is inconceivable that men trained in Judaism, like St Paul, in a system that rigorously forbade, under the severest penalties, human sacrifices, could have recognized in the human death of our blessed Lord the true fulfilment of the ancient sacrificial ritual. If the habits of thought they exhibit, and the phraseology they employ, 'emerged to view after a lapse of centuries, then,' as it has been pointedly remarked, 'they might well be set down to a gradual divergence from the original institution, or to an entire subversion of it. But there was no time for such a process of declension or overthrow. The men who so freely apply sacrificial language to the Eucharist had seen the Apostles, or their immediate successors, and to suppose that they misconceived the whole matter of Christ's action, is to suppose that Christianity was corrupted at its very foundation[1].'

To object to this that we do not find the words 'sacrifice' or 'atonement' distinctly employed by our Lord in His discourses with His apostles on the mo-

[1] Freeman's *Principles of Divine Service*, II. 92.

mentous purpose of His Death is, as we have already shown, to overlook the wisdom of that progressive teaching, whereby He prepared the minds of the Apostles for the abrogation of the Old Covenant, not by acts of authority or external decrees, but 'by *realizing the desire of salvation* shewn forth by its most characteristic institutions.' He, the Saviour of the world, 'made no formal profession of His intention to do what He has actually done, and is now doing, for its benefit. He did not plainly say that He had come to civilize rude nations, to humanise savages, to abrogate slavery, to abolish polygamy, to bring into disuse judicial torture, to rid cities of the sanguinary exhibitions of the amphitheatre, to break up caste, and to set men forward on the course of free and hopeful improvement, on terms of brotherhood. Christ said little of these purposes, great as they are; but now that we see what it is which His religion does for nations, when it is allowed to take its effect upon them in its own manner, we turn anew to the record of His sermons and parables, and there, without difficulty, we find the efficient principles of all these silent reforms, and can trace each of them separately to its source, in this or that word of power, precept, or instance[1].'

Similarly He made no formal profession of His intention to abolish sacrifices; He imposed upon His followers no specific injunctions that they must cease; He did not dogmatically institute a comparison between the

[1] *Restoration of Belief*, p. 315.

Mosaic ordinances and the sacrifice He was about to offer on the altar of His Cross; with solemn and majestic composure He *finished His work*, and He foreknew it would *draw all men unto Him;* He imposed nothing, but He fulfilled all things; He gave Himself, and the Old Covenant *vanished away.*

Will not this suffice? Shall we be still exacting? Shall we demand that the doctrine of His Sacrifice be set forth by Himself in set terms; that Apostles be called upon to hear these 'many things' He Himself said He had to say to them, *before* they were in a condition to hear them or interpret their meaning? Shall we claim that for our special behoof the very fundamental principle of His Divine mission be altered, that He proclaim decrees, and give *premature* utterance to formal and dogmatic statements?

Rather let us be satisfied with His own wise counsels. He *was made of a woman, made under the Law*[1]. He submitted to all its requirements, fulfilled all its ordinances, and then He gave Himself a *ransom for many*, a very *Paschal Lamb*, a *spotless victim.* He died. He rose again. And then they, who had been *slow of heart to believe all that Moses in the Law and the Prophets had spoken*[2], at length saw the deep meaning and significance of His Life and Death. The Spirit *took of the things of Christ, and shewed them unto them*, and their eyes were opened. They saw all they had only dimly conceived and groped after

[1] Gal. iv. 4. [2] Lk. xxiv. 25.

before. They recognised the true interpretation of those words, *Sacrifice and offering Thou didst not desire......burnt-offering and sin-offering hast Thou not required: then said I, Lo, I come*[1]. Like the two Apostles, to whom the Baptist pointed out the *Lamb of God*, they left the Type for the Antitype; that which was PERFECT was COME, that which was in PART was DONE AWAY.

[1] Ps. xl. 6; Heb. x. 6, 7.

CHAPTER IX.

THE EUCHARIST A SACRAMENT OF OUR REDEMPTION.

Cœna Domini est Sacramentum nostræ per mortem Christi Redemptionis.
ART. XXVIII.

WE have seen then that as the commemoration of a mere martyrdom, the institution of the Lord's Supper is inexplicable; that the Institutional words accompanying it are plainly sacrificial; that as a feast upon a sacrifice it was accepted and celebrated by the first disciples, who living in a sacrificial age had the best means of forming an opinion respecting its true character. This being so, the Lord's Supper is by its very nature a declaration on the part of our Lord Himself, of the utmost conceivable importance, that His death upon the cross was a *real sacrifice*, 'and not merely so called by conversion of terms or accommodation of ideas[1].'

Speaking of the doctrine of Election, it was the

[1] 'For figurative expressions (as some are apt to deem the Gospel representation of Christ's sacrifice and atonement) could never produce a religious Rite of Divine appointment, arising from, and dependent on, a real specific action.' Warburton's *Works*, Vol. v. p. 551.

remark of Bishop Ridley[1], 'in these matters I am so fearful that I dare not speak further, yea, almost none otherwise, than the very text doth, as it were, lead me by the hand.' These words fitly express the reverent and teachable spirit in which we should approach the consideration of the great doctrine of Christ's sacrifice, 'of that full, perfect, and sufficient sacrifice, oblation and satisfaction for the sins of the whole world' which He made once for all upon His cross. For no doctrine is more apt to suffer either from falling short of the *general* teaching of the Scriptures respecting it, or from narrowing our view to one out of the many various symbols and figures whereby it is there set forth[2].

Manifold, as we have already remarked, were the prophetic intimations to the Jewish Church, of the person and work of man's Deliverer. In the infancy of the world He was represented as the Bruiser of the Serpent's head[3]; to Abraham as the promised Seed in whom all nations of the earth should be blessed[4]; to Jacob as the Shiloh or Peace-Maker[5]; to David as the King that should sit upon his throne and of whose dominion there should be no end[6]; Isaiah spake of Him as the Prince of Peace, as the Virgin's Son[7], as a Man of sorrows and acquainted with grief[8]; Jere-

[1] Letter to Bradford, quoted in Bp. Browne *on the Articles*, p. 413.

[2] See Abp. Thomson's *Bampton Lectures*, p. 135; Swainson's *Hulsean Lectures*, p. 469.

[3] Gen. iii. 15.

[4] Gen. xii. 3; xviii. 18; xxii. 18.

[5] Gen. xlix. 10.

[6] 2 Sam. vii. 12—17; Psalm lxxxix. 29, 36.

[7] Isaiah vii. 14 and ix. 6.

[8] Isaiah liii. 3.

miah as the 'Lord our Righteousness[1];' Zechariah as the 'Priest-king[2];' Daniel as the 'Messiah to be cut off, but not for Himself[3]; Malachi as the 'Messenger of the Covenant[4],' and 'the Sun of righteousness arising with healing in his wings[5].

Similarly various we found to be the images employed in the Gospel narrative respecting the purport and object of His death. Slowly and gradually the truth included in the first announcement of the Angel to Joseph was developed, and men were prepared to apprehend it. The 'Saviour from sin,' the 'Lamb of God,' the 'Temple destroyed and raised again,' the 'uplifted Serpent,' the 'Bread of Life,' the good 'Shepherd giving his life for the sheep,' the 'Seed-corn dying before it can bring forth fruit,' the 'Ransom-money paid for the captive,' all these varied figures we have seen employed when the Holy One Himself, or men like His forerunner, would speak of His death, and the benefits He came to bestow upon the world.

Moreover in the more doctrinal portions of the New Testament we find the same variety of images and figures[6]. No system of morality, but the death of Christ 'for us men and for our salvation' was the uniform teaching of the Apostles to whomsoever they addressed themselves, the inhabitants of Jerusalem, or the Gentile Cornelius, in Galatia or Macedonia, at Athens or at Rome.

[1] Jer. xxiii. 6; xxxiii. 15, 16. [2] Zech. vi. 13.
[3] Dan. ix. 26. [4] Mal. iii. 1. [5] Mal. iv. 2.
[6] See Grotii *Defensio Fidei Catholicæ de Satisfactione Christi*, Cap. I. Works, Vol. III. p. 297.

Again, however, it is under no single figure, but with varied trains of association that the Apostles represent the effects of that death to our finite faculties. Did the Baptist speak to his two wondering disciples of the 'Lamb of God who should take away the sin of the world'? The same idea of the 'Lamb without blemish or spot' recurs once and again in the Epistles of St Peter[1]. Did the Saviour Himself suggest the idea of the 'Shepherd giving His life for the sheep'? The same idea recurs too often for us to enumerate in the Epistles, wherever He is said to have suffered 'for us, and in our stead[2].' Did the Saviour speak of His death under the figure of giving His life a ransom for many'? The idea of recall from captivity through a price paid is of frequent occurrence in the writings of St Paul. Did the Angel announce to Joseph the birth of One 'who should save his people from their sins,' and did the Holy One Himself, when He instituted the Eucharist, speak of His Blood as 'shed for many, for the remission of sins'? The same figure recurs in the Epistles of St John, when

[1] 1 Pet. i. 18, 19.

[2] On the force of ὑπέρ and ἀντί as applied in the N. T. to the Death of Christ, see Winer, *Grammar of the New Testament*, II. 401, and a quotation from Tischendorf's *Doctrina Pauli de vi mortis Christi satisfactoria*, quoted in Archbp. Trench's *N. T. Synonyms*, Part II. p. 147; Grotius, *De Satisfact. Christi*, c. 9; Bp Ellicott *on Gal.* III. 13. Winer, Trench, Tischendorf, Ellicott all agree that ὑπέρ has the signification of *in loco* as well as *in commodum* alicujus, that in doctrinal passages it may admit of the first meaning *united* with the second where the context seems to require it, but never has the first meaning *exclusively*. See also Bull *on Justification*, Part II. p. 239; *Library of Ang.-Cath. Theol.*

He speaks of Christ as 'the propitiation for our sins[1],' and says that 'His Blood cleanseth us from all sin[2];' of St Peter, when he affirms that He 'bore our sins in His own body on the tree[3];' of St Paul, when he declares that the Father made 'Him to be sin, or a sin-offering, for us, who knew no sin[4],' that we 'have redemption through His Blood, the remission of our sins,' that 'He gave Himself for us, that He might redeem us from all iniquity[5];' terms borrowed not more, as is often asserted, from the Mosaic sacrifices than from those which obtained universally throughout the ancient world. Lastly, did the Angelic Host on the world's first Christmas morn announce 'on earth peace, good will toward men[6],' and did the Saviour, in that momentous conversation with Nicodemus, to which we have already referred, declare that 'God so loved the world, that He gave His only begotten Son... not to condemn the world, but that the world through Him might be saved[7]'? What is this but the root-thought of that Reconciliation, that *At-one-ment*[8], which so often occurs in the Epistles of St Paul, as when he tells us that 'when we were enemies, we were recon-

[1] 1 Jn. ii. 2.

[2] 1 Jn. i. 7.

[3] 1 Pet. ii. 24. 'Hebræi ut significent quod Latini dicunt *pœnas pendere*, nullam habeat phrasim magis receptam quam hanc *ferre peccatum*, cui similis est Latinorum locutio, *luere delicta*, hoc est delictorum supplicia. Eadem plane phrasi dixit Petrus, Christum peccata nostra sursum tulisse in corpore suo in lignum.' Grotius, *Def. Fid. Cath. de Satisf. Christi*, c. 1.

[4] 2 Cor. v. 21.

[5] Titus ii. 14.

[6] Lk. ii. 14.

[7] Jn. iii. 16, 17.

[8] 'The *reconciliation* of two estranged parties was the earlier mean-

ciled to God through the death of His Son[1];' that through our Lord Jesus Christ 'we have received the atonement[2];' that in Christ God 'was reconciling the world unto Himself, not imputing their trespasses unto them[3];' that through Him the Father was pleased 'to reconcile all things unto Himself, having made peace through the Blood of His Cross[4]'?

Quotations to the same effect might be multiplied. But these are sufficient to show that the four great circles of images[5], which the Apostles employ when they seek to represent to us the effect of Christ's death, (1) a sin-offering, (2) reconciliation with an offended friend, (3) ransom or redemption from slavery, (4) satisfaction of a debt, *coincide with those employed by our Lord Himself in the Gospel Narrative.*

Following the example of Apostles and Evangelists, the Church of England in her Formularies and Articles similarly approaches the truth of Christ's sacri-

ing of the word atonement;' Archbp. Trench, *Glossary*, pp. 12, 13, who quotes

He and Aufidius can no more *atone*
Than violentest contrarieties.
Shakespeare, *Coriolanus*, Act IV. Sc. 6.

'His first essay succeeded so well, Moses would adventure on a second design, to *atone* two Israelites at variance.' T. Fuller, *Pisgah Sight of Palestine.*

[1] Rom. v. 10. [2] Rom. v. 11.

[3] 2 Cor. v. 18, 19. [4] Col. i. 20.

[5] See Grotii *Defensio Fidei Catholicæ de Satisfactione Christi*, Cap. I.; Coleridge's *Aids to Reflection*, I. 259; Archbp. Trench's *New Testament Synonyms*, Part II. p. 120; Dean Goodwin's *Hulsean Lectures*, p. 221.

fice from several different quarters, and uses a similar variety of expressions in setting forth a doctrine which in all its length and breadth and depth and height transcends the limits of our comprehension. Thus while in the Apostles' Creed we are simply taught to say that Jesus Christ 'suffered under Pontius Pilate,' in the Nicene we add that 'for us men and for our salvation He came down from heaven, was made man, and crucified for us.' In other places we are taught that 'Christ is the very Paschal Lamb, which was offered for us, and hath taken away the sin of the world[1];' that 'very God and very Man, He truly suffered, was crucified, died, and was buried, to reconcile His Father to us, and to be a sacrifice, not only for original guilt, but also for all actual sins of men[2];' that the offering of Christ once made is a 'perfect redemption, propitiation, and satisfaction for all the sins of the whole world, both original and actual[3];' that 'by His meritorious Cross and Passion alone we obtain remission of our sins and are made partakers of the kingdom of heaven[4];' that 'of His tender love toward mankind God sent His Son to take upon Him our flesh, and to suffer death upon the cross[5];' 'to die for our sins, and to rise

[1] *Communion Office*, Proper Preface for Easter Day; comp. Article XV.

[2] Article II.

[3] Article XXXI. On the word *satisfaction*, which again occurs in the Collect for the 4th Sunday in Advent, and dates from the writings of Archbp. Anselm, see Swainson's *Hulsean Lectures*, p. 283, and the notes. Thomson's *Bampton Lectures*, p. 134.

[4] *Comm. Office.*

[5] Collect for Sunday before Easter.

again for our justification[1];' that 'God the Son hath redeemed us and all mankind[2].'

But whatever be the metaphors by which we illustrate the consequences of Christ's sacrifice on His Cross, whether it be that of reconciliation with an offended friend, or redemption from slavery, or the satisfaction of a debt, or a sin-offering, the Sacrament of the Lord's Supper, by its very nature, being a religious Rite of Divine appointment and dependent on a real specific action, is a declaration of Jesus Himself that His death was a real sacrifice[3].

For, to quote again the words of our Articles and Formularies, the Supper of the Lord is 'not only a sign of the love that Christians ought to have among themselves one to another, but rather a Sacrament of our Redemption by Christ's death: insomuch that to such as rightly, worthily, and with faith, receive the same, the Bread which we break is a partaking of the Body of Christ; and likewise the Cup of Blessing is a partaking of the Blood of Christ[4];' it is 'a Holy Mystery instituted and

[1] Collect for 1st Sunday after Easter.

[2] Catechism. Compare the Homily of the Salvation of all Mankind and the two Homilies on the Passion.

[3] This view has never been wanting in any age of Christianity. 'Even the Jewish Christians were more and more definitely forced on this, while the Ebionites mutilated also the Supper.' Dorner's *Person of Christ*, I. 167. E. T. 'Already in the days of the Apostles there had arisen those who denied that Jesus Christ was come in the flesh, or that there was any resurrection from the dead. But none called in question the reality of Christ's sacrifice of Himself *on the ground of its being a sacrifice*, or stumbled at any other sacrificial feature of the system.' Freeman's *Principles of Divine Service*, II. 90, 91.

[4] Article XXVIII.

ordained by our Master and only Saviour Jesus Christ, to the end that we should alway remember His exceeding great love in dying for us, and the innumerable benefits which by His precious blood-shedding He hath obtained to us[1];' it is a 'pledge of His love[2];' it is a 'certain sure witness,' an outward, visible, and '*effectual* sign of God's good will towards us[3];' an assurance that a reconciliation of man to God has been effected, that a ransom has been paid, that an all-perfect and sufficient sacrifice for sin has been offered, so that each faithful recipient can 'take and eat' the Bread 'in remembrance that Christ died for *him*,' that 'the Body of our Lord Jesus Christ was given for *him*,' and can drink of the Cup 'in remembrance that Christ's blood was shed for *him*[4].'

The Lord's Supper, then, is not only a feast upon a Sacrifice, but by its very nature a *seal* and *pledge* of reconciliation.

In all ages, God, in His infinite mercy has been wont to speak to man not only in words but in outward and symbolical actions. He is no hard taskmaster, 'He knoweth whereof we are made,' that we are not pure spirit, but bear about with us bodies also; that from the weakness of our mortal nature we cannot always

1 *Communion Office.* 2 Ibid.

3 Art. xxv. 'Panis et Vini symbolis nobis confirmatur Christi corpus ...ut reconciliationem gratiæ *ad nos pertinere certo sciamus, fructumque redemptionis per mortem ejus partæ capiamus atque percipiamus.*' Nowell's *Catechism*, p. 93; Parker Soc. Ed. *Homily Concerning the Sacrament*, p. 447; Corrie's Edition.

4 *Communion Office.*

stand upright, or stay ourselves utterly on Him. The language of men in all ages has been that of the Patriarch, 'Lord God, whereby shall I *know* that I shall inherit it[1]?' And, in condescension to the want thus expressed, the all-merciful God has ever been wont to confirm His word with some pledge or sign[2].

The Rainbow after the flood[3]; the smoking furnace and the burning lamp that passed between the divided victims before Abraham[4]; the signs given to Moses when he was afraid to go before Pharaoh[5]; the blood sprinkled on book, people, and altar, when the Covenant was ratified at Sinai[6]; these are only a few instances out of many where God has condescended to human weakness, and by external pledges assured them of the certainty of His promises.

But however needful may have been those pledges vouchsafed on the occasions just mentioned, it needs but a passing contemplation of those deep wants which found an expression in the ancient sacrificial system, to

[1] Gen. xv. 8.

[2] See Swainson's *Hulsean Lectures*, p. 213. Thomson's *Bampton Lectures*, p. 227.

[3] Gen. ix. 13. [4] Gen. xv. 1—21. [5] Exod. iv. 1—3.

[6] Exod. xxiv. 6—8. 'Nos quidem mente, atque intelligentia adeo cœlesti Divinaque non sumus, ut nobis Angelorum instar Divinæ gratiæ pure per se appareant; hac ergo ratione infirmitati nostræ consuluit Deus, ut qui terreni sumus atque cæci, in externis elementis et figuris, quasi speculis quibusdam, cœlestes gratias, quas alioqui non cerneremus, intueremur; et id nostra maxime refert, ut sensibus etiam nostris Dei promissiones ingerantur, quo mentibus nostris sine ulla dubitatione confirmantur.' Nowell's *Catechism*, Parker Soc. Ed. p. 84; Nicholson *on the Catechism*, p. 189.

perceive the inestimable value of this Sacrament, if only we consider it from this single point of view as a pledge of God's love and goodwill towards us, as an outward and visible sign 'of our redemption by Christ's death.'

For the question, which in all ages man has felt to concern himself most nearly, is, 'How do I stand in reference to that Being of whose greatness, goodness, and power I cannot but be sensible as often as I reflect on the various phenomena of the physical world, and how does He stand affected towards me?'

If he attempt to answer this question from a renewed reflection on the external world, what does he perceive? That in this world of order[1] there is disorder of the most extensive kind. There is pain; there is suffering; there is universal liability to disease; there is the famine and the plague; and then there is death, the solemn silence of the tomb[2].

Nay more, the faculty of Conscience, which strengthens so mightily man's religious instinct, testifies to a deep-seated source of disorder *within himself*, to a schism *in his own soul*. Man feels he is not as he ought to be, or as he was intended to have been[3].

For sin has never reigned with such entirely undisputed sway over man's heart, but there have been

[1] Compare the names Κόσμος and *mundus* which the two most cultivated nations of the ancient world applied to the universe. Humboldt's *Cosmos*, I. 51. n; also the dialogue of Socrates with Aristodemus, Xen. *Mem.* I. 4; Cicero, *de Nat. Deor.* II. 49—61.

[2] For illustrations of the conviction of the general misery of man amongst the Greeks, see Döllinger, *Jew and Gentile*, I. 294.

[3] See Ackermann's *Christian Element in Plato*, p. 203.

voices protesting against its lordship, and witnessing against it as an alien and a usurper[1]. Conscience may not be sovereign *de facto*, but *de jure* it is felt to be.

It was the sense of this inward derangement, this bondage[2] of the will to some mysterious and opposing power, which made one of the ancient heathens exclaim that 'he felt as if two souls were lodged within him.' 'What is it,' writes another to a friend, 'which drags me this way when I wish to go that? What is it that is ever wrestling with our will, nor suffers us once and for ever to desire the same thing[3]?' Another[4], and he one of the wisest of men that ever lived before the Advent, could only express his sense of the struggle within him by speaking of the soul as a 'chariot, which two horses, one white and one black, were dragging in different directions.' The well-known lines of the frivolous and worldly Ovid,

> Video meliora proboque
> Deteriora sequor,

express the feelings of every man that ever lived, and testify alike to the all-attractive loveliness of virtue, and the deep conviction of personal shortcoming[5].

[1] On the Platonic doctrine of Sin, see Ackermann, 58, and notes.

[2] 'Quis neget omnes improbos esse servos?' Cicero. *'Ελευθερία καὶ δουλεία, τὸ μὲν ἀρετῆς ὄνομα, τὸ δὲ κακίας.* Epictetus.

[3] Seneca, *Epist.* LII; Conf. Xenophon, *Cyrop.* VI. I. 41.

[4] Plato, *Phædrus*, 246.

[5] With Plato Virtue is health, beauty (*Rep.* IV. 444. e), and harmony of soul (*Gorg.* 482. b), while the effects of sin he considers as afflictive and as corrupting; for he says that sin renders the soul sick and ugly, and reduces it to slavery (*Rep.* IV. 444. c; IX. 579. d. Comp. St

Combined with this sense of internal weakness there is a sense also of unmeetness to enter into God's presence. Man feels that God is very near to him in the operations of His hands, and in the voice of conscience, but he is afraid to draw very near to Him. 'Be he brave or be he timid, in one respect he is the same, he dares not to stand by himself. If he believes in God at all, if he is not a thoroughly convinced atheist, his heart will either rise in prayer or sink in imprecations. But whether he prays or curses, the witness is the same, wrung out from the inmost depths of his being: and that witness is that he is unfit, and knows himself to be unfit, to stand upright in his own strength before God[1].' In the midst of outward pleasures and happiness there is in the breast of thousands a sorrow which knows no joy, an inward grief, an indefinable sense of defect, all the more dreadful because it is so indefinable.

But what does man say to these things? Does he give up all hope of deliverance and salvation? The answer to this is inscribed in an emphatic negative on the pages of history. Never has the mind of man, driven to construct a form of worship even from its natural promptings, invented a *religion of despair*. He has ever believed that the great gulf which separates him from the Supreme may be bridged over, that the sense of guilt which causes such indefinable fear may be

John viii. 34); it robs man of his fairest joys here and of heavenly bliss hereafter; the impure and unholy cannot come to God (*Phæd.* 69. c). Ackermann, 59, and notes; and comp. Döllinger, I. 321.

[1] Swainson's *Hulsean Lectures* in 1848 and 1858, p. 61.

removed. And wherever there has been a sense of repentance, a sorrow for sin, there has been also a belief in the necessity of something to be done *for* man and not *by* man, if the broken relations between himself and his Maker are to be renewed.

Now of this deepfelt sense of the need of reconciliation, sacrifice has ever been the outward expression[1]. Whatever may be our opinions respecting its origin, whether we believe it to have been invented by man for himself, or to have been taught him by external revelation, certain it is that it has universally prevailed. It is no mere Jewish notion. For four thousand years it prevailed before the Advent, among nations widely sundered from the Jews in everything else. However far apart they might be in other respects, in this at least they were at one, in the conviction that there was something which hindered man's free access to the Deity without an intermediary; and all that we know, independently of Revelation, of sin, in ourselves, in savage tribes, or at certain epochs in national history[2], only tends to shew how true this sense was, and how awful a thing sin is.

[1] The fact that in the face of the natural law *the soul that sinneth it shall die*—every nation visited death upon sinless victims, in order to extirpate its own transgressions, will be taken by any candid persôn as a sign that the principle of sacrifice has a stronger hold on the human mind than that of simple retribution. Archbp. Thomson's *Bampton Lectures*, p. 32. The prodigality of the sacrifices offered up by the Emperor Julian, which gained him the title of *Victimarius*, and his submission even to the loathsome tauroboliad, after renouncing Christianity, is very striking. See Smith's *Gibbon*, III. 148.

[2] For illustrations see Ackermann, pp. 195, 196.

Now, so long as this sense of inherent impurity, of internal derangement, of guilt, has no adequate source of relief, there can be no real peace. For the side of human life most full of suffering and evil is the religious side; it is here that the virus of the disease has its chief seat. By its repeated confessions of the dream-like nothingness of its own glory, by its constant complaints of the impossibility of the things of time and sense *entirely* to satisfy its longings, by its inability to rid itself of the consciousness of shortcoming, by its ten thousand times ten thousand instances since the world began of agonized remorse, by the terrible 'earnestness of its guilt-offerings, its punishments, penances, and self-tortures[1],' the world testifies, and has testified from the beginning, to the existence within it of some profound source of misery, and cries with the Apostle, *O wretched man that I am! who shall deliver me from the body of this death*[2]*?*

And it is to this malady that the Gospel addresses itself. It does not mock man by telling him that he is deceiving himself, that the disease, to which his own bitter experience only too surely testifies, is a creature of his imagination. It does not mock him, as some human systems have done, by bidding him be comfortable, and regard his consciousness of demerit as a shadow. What philosophy lays down as the ultimate difficulty, the enigma of all enigmas, the existence of sin, with this the Gospel starts. 'In this darkness, or this

[1] Ackermann, 206. [2] Rom. vii. 24.

light of nature, call it which you please, Revelation comes in, confirms every doubting fear which could enter into the heart of man concerning the future unprevented consequence of wickedness; supposes the world to be in a state of ruin (a supposition which seems the very ground of the Christian dispensation, and which, if not provable by reason, yet is in no wise contrary to it); teaches us too, that the rules of Divine government are such, as not to admit of pardon immediately and directly on repentance, or by the sole efficacy of it: but then teaches, at the same time, what nature might justly have hoped, that the moral government of the universe was not so rigid, but that there was room for an interposition to avert the fatal consequences of vice, which, therefore, by this means, does admit of pardon. Revelation teaches us, that the unknown laws of God's more general government, no less than the particular laws by which we experience He governs us at present, are compassionate, as well as good in the more general notion of goodness: and that He hath mercifully provided that there should be an interposition to prevent the destruction of human kind, whatever that destruction unprevented would have been[1].'

For in His tender love to mankind the Father sent the Son into the world. The purport of His coming is declared on the very first page of the Gospel narrative to be 'the saving of His people from their

[1] Butler's *Analogy*, Part II. chap. 5.

sins.' To effect this deliverance He took upon Him our nature, entered into conflict with the Evil One, and proved Himself victorious over the worst enemies of man's happiness, over disease, over death, over that world of spiritual foes with which man in all ages has believed that the human race has become entangled. He 'republished to men the law of nature, which men had corrupted; and the very knowledge of which, to some degree, was lost among them;' He deepened the requirements of the moral law, and so rectified the aberrations of conscience; He closed His earthly ministry by freely and spontaneously giving Himself up to death, even the death of the Cross, for man and in man's stead. He died, He was buried, He rose again, He ascended into heaven, there to carry on before His Father's throne that work of mediation and priestly intercession which man in all ages has felt he needed. And before He left the world He instituted a Holy Mystery as a visible pledge of His love, 'for a continual remembrance of His death,' and of 'the innumerable benefits which by His precious Blood-shedding He hath obtained to us[1].'

Every time, then, that we listen to the words of Institution, which He uttered on the night that He was betrayed; every time that we draw near and receive the symbols of His Body broken, and His Blood poured out, we have signed and sealed to each one of us the pledge of our Redemption by His death, and 'before

[1] *Communion Office.*

our eyes He is evidently set forth crucified[1]' for us. Every time that we approach this Feast upon the one full, perfect, and sufficient sacrifice, and oblation, once offered for the sins of the whole world, and think of HIM who offered it, who was with the Father before all worlds, 'God of God, Light of Light, very God of very God,' 'by whom all things were made,' but who for our sakes came down from heaven, and satisfied for us and as our Head 'the Divine craving and yearning after a perfect holiness, righteousness, and obedience,' the shadows that hide the face of God flee away, and we *know* and are *assured* that we are not living in a redeemerless world, that One has come and reconciled us to God, and that we need not 'look for another.'

And reflecting on His infinite love, and receiving its seals and pledges, we are not concerned to explain how and in what particular way 'His sacrifice of Himself had that efficacy for obtaining pardon of sin, which the heathens may be supposed to have thought their sacrifices to be, and which the Jewish sacrifices really were in some degree, and with regard to some persons[2].' Scripture has left 'this matter of the satisfaction of Christ, mysterious, left somewhat in it unrevealed;' nor can we show any claim to further explanation. We know that sin itself still remains an enigma

[1] Gal. iii. 1. 'Tantum dicimus, quemadmodum *fides* est quasi *manus nostra*, qua nos quærimus et accipimus; sic *verbum* et *sacramenta* esse quasi *manus Dei*, quibus is nobis offert et confert quod fide a nobis petitur et accipitur.' Vossius, *de Sacram. Vi et Effic.* quoted in Waterland, *Works*, IX. 435.

[2] Butler's *Analogy*, II. 5. Waterland's *Works*, Vol. IX. 393.

which we can see but cannot explain; we know that on vicarious suffering the whole world is built up, that 'in lower forms,—not low in themselves,—though low as compared with the highest,—it is everywhere, where love is at all[1]; we know that the mystery of sacrifice is the condition of the support of even our daily lives, nay, that the death of man is often the condition of the life of his fellow man; we know that *except a corn of wheat fall into the ground and die, it abideth alone, but if it die it bringeth forth much fruit;*' and we remember who it was that suggested this analogy, and are content to leave the matter[2] in His hands, convinced that to object to the 'principle of mediation is to object to the whole daily course of Divine Providence in the government of the world.'

[1] Trench's *University Sermons*, p. 33.

[2] 'Of the dark parts of revelation,' says Warburton, 'there are two sorts: one which may be cleared up by the studious application of well employed talents; the other, which will always reside within the shadow of God's throne, where it would be impiety to intrude.' 'The great Atonement—who shall dare to say that he knows enough of the counsels of heaven, the requisitions of God, and His relation to man—to pronounce it *improbable?* Who is he that comes among us in the high character of confidential secretary to the Divine administration, that he can venture to affirm that God requires no suffering Mediator?' Archer Butler's *Sermons*, I. 263.

CPSIA information can be obtained
at www.ICGtesting.com
Printed in the USA
LVHW111638170422
716440LV00006B/618